JOE COLTON'S JOURNAL

I'm still reeling from the bombshell that all these months my "wife" was really Meredith's psychotic identical twin sister, Patsy Portman! It makes me see red every time I think about this evil impostor taking over my wife's life while the real Meredith was struggling to get back to me. Yet there was a part of me that always felt in my heart that the woman who was under my roof was not my life's companion and soul mate. Finally being able to hold my cherished wife in my arms again was pure bliss.... Unfortunately, a dark cloud shadows my adopted daughter's happy homecoming. Emily feels responsible for the death of Toby Atkins, who gave his life protecting her during this entire Patsy debacle. Now his revenge-seeking older brother, Josh, has arrived in Prosperino and is making ridiculous accusations against sweet Emily. But underneath the bitter animosity between Emily and Josh is a smoldering attraction that can't be denied. Could there be wedding bells in their future?

About the Author

KASEY MICHAELS

is a *New York Times* and *USA Today* bestselling author of more than sixty books that range from contemporary to historical romance. Recipient of the Romance Writers of America RITA Award and a Career Achievement Award from *Romantic Times Magazine*, in addition to writing for Harlequin and Silhouette, Kasey is currently writing single-title contemporary fiction and Regency historical romances elsewhere. When asked about her work for THE COLTONS series, she said that she has rarely felt so involved in a project, one with such scope and diversity of plot and characters.

Kasey Michaels

The Hopechest Bride

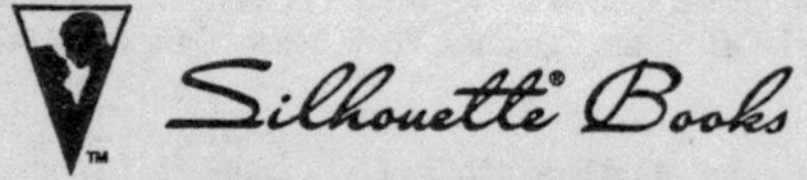

Published by Silhouette Books
America's Publisher of Contemporary Romance

Special thanks and acknowledgment are given to Kasey Michaels for her contribution to THE COLTONS series.

SILHOUETTE BOOKS
300 East 42nd St.,
New York, N. Y. 10017

ISBN 0-373-38715-6

THE HOPECHEST BRIDE

This edition published by arrangement with Harlequin Books S.A.

Visit Silhouette at www.eHarlequin.com

Printed in U.S.A.

THE COLTONS

Meet the Coltons—
a California dynasty with a legacy of privilege and power.

Emily Blair: *The younger woman.* Though his brother was killed in the line of duty while protecting her, she thinks that the only thing Josh Atkins wants from her is revenge.

Josh Atkins: *The older man.* He'd come to Prosperino to get even with the cold, heartless witch who had lured his naive brother into a trap. But as he gets to know this sweet, warmhearted woman, could his mission be changing to marriage?

Jewel Mayfair: *The love child.* Having been found by a private investigator, this psychologist is sad to learn about her mother, Patsy, but welcomes the chance to meet her Colton cousins....

Patsy Portman: *The deranged sibling.* Now that the jig is up, the real Meredith turns out to be Patsy's true champion by finding a good lawyer for her unstable twin.

THE COLTONS

Theodore Colton m. 1940 Kay Barkley
1908–1954 1919–1954

Ed Barkley m. 1916 Betty Barkley
1895–1966 1899–1970

Edna Kelly m. 1945 George Portman
1920–1970 1915–

Patsy
1949–

Meredith Portman
1949–

m. 1969

Joseph Colton
1941–

Graham Colton
1946–

m. 1970

Cynthia Turner
1941–

Jackson, 1973–
Liza, 1975–

- Jewel, 1969–
  (by Ellis Mayfair)
- *Joe, Jr., 1991–
- *Teddy, Jr., 1993–

Natural Children

- Rand, 1970–
- Drake, 1972–
  Michael, 1972–1980
- Sophie, 1974–
- Amber, 1976–

Foster Children

- Chance Reilly, 1967–
- Tripp Calhoun, 1968–
- Rebecca Powell, 1968–
- Wyatt Russell, 1969–
- Blake Fallon, 1969–
- River James, 1970–
- *Emily Blair, 1980–

THE McGRATHS

Jack McGrath
1906–1988

m. 1935

Maureen O'Toole
1915–1989

Liam, 1936–
Collin, 1938–
Maude, 1940–
Francis, 1942–
Peter m. 1970 Andie Clifton
1949– 1951–

Austin, 1971–
Heather, 1976–

LEGEND
--- Child of Affair
▬ Twins
* Adopted by Joe Colton

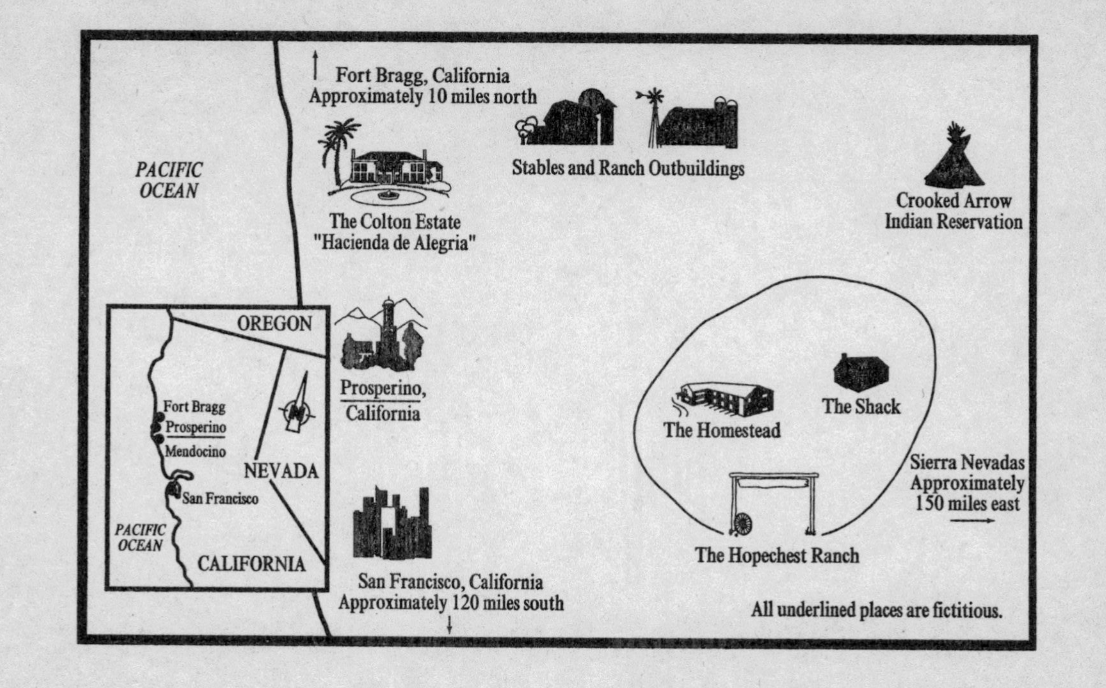
PACIFIC OCEAN
Fort Bragg, California
Approximately 10 miles north
The Colton Estate
"Hacienda de Alegria"
Stables and Ranch Outbuildings
Crooked Arrow
Indian Reservation
OREGON
NEVADA
CALIFORNIA
Fort Bragg
Prosperino
Mendocino
San Francisco
PACIFIC OCEAN
Prosperino,
California
San Francisco, California
Approximately 120 miles south
The Homestead
The Shack
The Hopechest Ranch
Sierra Nevadas
Approximately
150 miles east
All underlined places are fictitious.

San Francisco Gazette
BULLETIN
A Tale of Two Wives

Former Senator Joseph Colton, Wife and Family Live Decade-long Nightmare

by Wanda Harris

(Prosperino; AP) The sleepy town of Prosperino, California woke to a nightmare this morning as it was revealed that esteemed former Senator Joseph Colton has been the victim of a ten-year-long impersonation and tragic hoax that has all but shattered the prosperous Colton family.

Colton, head of Colton Enterprises, has lately been in the national news after two unsuccessful attempts on his life, attempts made allegedly by a disgruntled former business associate, Emmett Fallon. Fallon is now under arrest and awaiting trial.

Details of this new revelation as concerns Joseph Colton remain sketchy, but Detective Thaddeus Law of the Prosperino Police Department has confirmed that one Patricia Portman, a convicted murderer, had somehow taken the place of her identical twin sister,

Meredith Portman Colton, wife of the former senator. Portman successfully impersonated her sister over the course of a decade, until her true identity was revealed upon yesterday's return of Meredith Colton.

Meredith Colton, well-known in the Prosperino area for her various charitable works, has spent that decade in an as yet unidentified locale, reportedly a victim of amnesia. This amnesia, a highly-placed source in the police department reports, made it easy for Portman to slip into her sister's life at the family estate, the Hacienda de Alegria.

For those ten years, Portman was, to family and community, Meredith Colton, and bore Joseph Colton one child, a son, Teddy, age eight. The Senator, however, has been ruled out as a possible willing co-conspirator, and there are, at this time, no plans to indict him along with Portman.

Portman, soon to be indicted for, as Law stated, "a laundry list of charges," is currently being held for questioning at the county jail. Although Law refused to comment further, other sources report that attempted murder and fraud charges are being prepared, with an arraignment to be held at an undisclosed time, possibly as early as this afternoon.

The more bizarre aspects of this case, and there are many, have caused national attention to be drawn to Prosperino and the Colton ranch, attention that will not soon fade.

(Related stories and photos on the Colton family, holdings and history in Section B, page 1; see TWO WIVES)

One

Joe Colton threw down the newspaper in obvious disgust, and turned to glare at his oldest son. ''All right. Who the hell is this Wanda Harris, and who did she talk to out of Law's office? Damn it, Rand, I can't believe this. It has only been twenty-four hours, and the wire services have already picked up on the story. I can have the phones controlled here at the ranch, but we're going to have a million reporters camping outside the gates like damned vultures! Trucks. Lights. Satellite dishes. Idiots trying to breach the fences. Your mother can't handle this, Rand. We've got to do something.''

Rand bent to pick up the newspaper, laid it on the desk in Joe's study. ''Dad, speaking as an attorney now, there's only so much we can do. Freedom of the press, and all of that.''

Joe wasn't listening. He was too busy pacing, hands clenched into fists, talking to himself. ''And Teddy! Damn it, why did she have to mention Teddy? And to say I won't be indicted? Indicted for what? Would anyone actually *believe* that I would have been a willing partner in Patsy's scheme? Hell, obviously that reporter did. She wondered enough to ask the question and print an answer. Because of Teddy, I suppose. What a mess. Harris is making it all sound like some kind of tabloid scandal.''

Rand rubbed at the bridge of his nose and winced. ''Yeah, I know. It was bad enough when the news came out about Emmett, but this one *does* have all the makings of a tabloid feeding frenzy. You can keep it low-key on Colton Enterprises stations, and my cousin Harrison won't allow anything sensational in his publications—but this definitely is not going to go away overnight, Dad. You're a former senator and business magnate, your sister-in-law unbelievably impersonated your wife for ten long years, you fathered her child—''

''I did *not*— Oh, God,'' Joe said, collapsing into the huge leather chair behind his desk. He took a deep breath, let it out slowly as he looked at his son. ''Teddy's not my child, Rand,'' he said carefully, looking toward the shut door to the hall. ''And that's when I should have known. She—Patsy—came to me, all excited, telling me she was pregnant, but I knew that wasn't possible. I knew I was sterile, and had been since that bout of mumps years ago. Your mother and I learned that when we tried to conceive after Michael's death and couldn't. But Patsy didn't know. I should have known then, *sensed* something then. Teddy's eight. This mess lasted eight more years than it should have. If only I hadn't forgiven Patsy, believed that she'd made a mistake, had a short affair because I wasn't...because I wasn't paying her enough attention, meeting her needs. God, you're right. The whole thing *does* sound like fodder for the tabloids."

His son remained silent for some moments, lost in his own thoughts, then asked, "Who is the father? Do you know?"

Joe shook his head. "No, and I don't think I want to know."

"Teddy might want to know," Rand put in tightly, avoiding his father's gaze.

Joe pushed back his chair, stood up. "Not now, Rand, don't go all ethical on me now. I can't think about Teddy's parentage now. I can't think about that, or the fact that your mother, when she saw Teddy and Joe, Jr. last night, remarked on how they looked very much like brothers. Because if I were to think that Joe is also— No. Like I said, I can't think about any of this now, about how blind I was, about the mistakes that were made. All I can do is protect your mother, Rand. We *all* have to protect your mother."

"That's a given, Dad," Rand said, walking over to the window and looking out into the courtyard, to where Teddy and ten-year-old Joe, Jr. were kicking a soccer ball. "Joe showed up on our doorstep, just an infant, only shortly before Mom's accident, remember? Just before Patsy took Mom's place here at the ranch. We all know how crazy Patsy is about Joe, about Teddy. It was almost as if the rest of her children, natural, adopted and foster children, were cut out of her life, leaving just those two boys. Could it be? Is it possible that Patsy left Joe on our doorstep, then arranged to move in herself and mother her child?"

Rand turned away from the window and looked at his father. "I think we need DNA tests, Dad. I think we need to know exactly what went on when Joe came to us. For Joe's sake. And if Teddy isn't to grow up believing you to be his father, maybe we need DNA testing on him, too. The last thing we need in this house, Dad, are more secrets."

Joe slowly nodded his head. "I'll talk to your mother, see what she wants to do. But not yet, Rand. She's too overwhelmed as it is, and very worried about Emily."

"We're all worried about Emily, and I've been giving something some thought for a few days now, even before we all came here to the ranch. I know I'm rushing things here, but I watched Emily when we were with Mom's psychologist in Mississippi. Dr. Martha Wilkes—a good, caring woman Mom really trusted. I was thinking, Dad, maybe we could get Dr. Wilkes to come out here for a while, stay at the ranch? Talk Mom past this media circus we're sure to have, help her adjust? And maybe talk with Emily while she's at it?''

''It's one step,'' Joe agreed, sighing. ''We have to start somewhere, don't we? God knows I feel the need to do *something*. Go ahead, Rand, call the doctor and see if she's agreeable. We'll pay all her expenses, of course, and have her here as our guest. And after that, find out if we can visit Patsy at the jail later today. I have some questions for her, and possibly a deal to make with the woman.''

Once upon a time there had been a small toddler-aged girl who was placed in the foster system after the deaths of her parents.

And once upon a time a fairy princess and her big, handsome prince had rescued that little girl from the system, taken her into their fairy-tale palace and raised her as their own. Adopted her, gave her their name while preserving the name of her parents, making sure the little girl still saw her grandmother while that good woman was alive.

Once upon a time that little girl was happy, loved, cherished. She lived in the fairy-tale palace, surrounded by foster and adopted brothers and sisters, adored by her new parents.

And then, when the girl, Emily Blair Colton, was eleven, the wicked witch destroyed all that happiness.

One fateful day, as Emily's adoptive mother, Meredith Colton, drove the child toward town, to visit her grandmother, there was an accident. A planned accident that drove Meredith's car off the road, tumbled it into a ditch.

Meredith was knocked unconscious, as was Emily, and when Emily awoke, still strapped into the seat belt in the back seat, she saw *two* mommies. Her good mommy, and the evil mommy. The wicked witch. Frightened as only an eleven-year-old could be, Emily fainted, and woke much later in the hospital, to see just one mommy.

But which mommy?

Not *her* mommy. Oh, no. Her real mommy would never yell at her, put a hand across her mouth to stop her from crying. Her real mommy wouldn't have somehow changed from laughing and loving to cold and accusing. Her real mommy would call her "Sparrow," and read her stories each night, and never yell, never call her "you bad, bad child."

Ten years. Ten long, dark years the wicked witch had stayed and the good mommy had been gone. Lost.

Nobody listened, nobody believed. Or did they? Someone finally had believed Emily. Someone had believed her enough to try to kill her, here at the ranch, here in her own bedroom. Someone had felt it necessary to shut up the child who was now a woman, yet still also the child who questioned, who still believed her good mommy had been stolen away by the wicked witch.

Because of that somebody, Emily had nearly died. Three times. And somebody *had* died, had died protecting her, had died saving her...had died loving her.

"It's my fault," Emily said aloud in her quiet bedroom, the yellow November sun slanting through the windows, onto her coverlet. "Toby's dead, and it's all my fault."

Detective Thaddeus Law pushed a fresh cup of coffee across the scarred wooden table, then waited as Patsy Portman lifted the cup and drank deeply. A department video camera perched on a tripod in a corner of the room was loaded with a fresh tape and ready to go after their lunch break, which had just ended. He hit the remote button, starting the machine, then once more recited his name, Patsy's name, the date, the place, the time. Once more he read Patsy Portman her Miranda rights, which she once again agreed to waive.

Everything was set, ready. He looked to his left, at the two-way mirror, and nodded. He'd begin now, ask the questions the men behind that two-way mirror had suggested.

Patsy Portman was dressed in the royal blue T-shirt and scrub pants imprinted with "Prosperino Jail" on the shirt back and one pants leg. Yet she still held her head high, her perfectly combed hair and makeup-free but still classically beautiful face so at odds with her attire, as were her carefully manicured fingernails.

It was only her eyes that told the true story of Patsy Portman. Those flat, dead eyes that could flash manic in an instant. Those eyes that held so many secrets, so much sorrow...and more than a hint of madness. She'd asked for her pills, twice, then refused to tell

Thaddeus where they were, who had prescribed them. Without her medication, the thin veil of sanity was rapidly slipping away.

The door to the interrogation room opened and Sgt. Kade Lummus stepped inside, clad in his sharply creased navy uniform pants, his crisply starched dark gray department-issue shirt. "Her lawyer's here," he said with a tip of his head toward the hallway. "You want me to send him in?"

"I don't need a lawyer," Patsy said, glaring at Thaddeus. "I've done nothing wrong. *Nothing.* I'm the victim here, remember." Her left eyelid began to twitch, but she kept her hands carefully folded on the edge of the table. Tightly folded, her knuckles white with strain. She was holding on, but she'd soon crack, go to pieces or to a place inside her mind where nobody could reach her.

It was now or never, Thaddeus decided, as soon they'd get nothing from the Portman woman. He looked toward the mirror once more. "Send him in, Kade, and then join us. Ms. Portman," he continued, leaning his elbows on the tabletop, "I know you waived your Miranda rights. You waived them several times, in fact. But even the innocent are advised to accept the services of a lawyer, and Mr. Roberts is one of the best defense attorneys in the state."

Patsy gave a toss of her head. "Sure. And who's paying him? *Joe?* The man's demented, lost his mind. Why not just lock me up and throw away the key? And my name is Colton, Thaddeus. Meredith Colton. I was a guest at your wedding, remember? I believe we gave you crystal. Baccarrat crystal. Do try to keep that straight in your head, all right?''

"Kade,'' Thad called out as the door opened once more and attorney Jim Roberts entered the room, Gucci briefcase in hand. "Three more coffees, if you please. This is going to take a while.''

"Ms. Portman,'' Attorney Roberts said after introducing himself, "I'm advising you not to say another word until we've been able to confer. And I'd like to have you examined by a psychiatrist as soon as possible.''

"Why? Because Joe says I'm nuts? Oh, yeah, he'd love that, wouldn't he? He'd just *love* that. You'd all love that.'' Patsy shook her head, then glared up at the attorney, her eyes spitting fire. "No deal. No shrinks. Bring one in here and I'll have the cops throw out the both of you. I can do that, you know. I have my rights.''

"Yes, you do, Patsy. You do have rights. So let's forget the doctor for the moment. We'll take this one step at a time. Detective Law?'' the attorney asked, looking at Thad. "I'd like a few moments alone with my client.''

"I am *not* your client,'' Patsy said angrily. "There is no way in *hell* I'm going to let Joe Colton pick my lawyer.'' She shook her head, laughed, a hint of the mania Thad had already glimpsed creeping into her voice. "Man, then I *would* be nuts, wouldn't I?'' She closed her eyes tightly for a moment, her face contorted, before her features smoothed once again. "Oh, hell, why not? Thaddeus, take a hike why don't you, and we'll see what Joe's offering. He *is* offering something, isn't he? They always do…they always do…they always— What? You're waiting for a bus, Thaddeus? Get out of here!''

Roberts gave a small jerk of his head, indicating that Thad should leave the room, which he did after switching off the video camera, going to join Joe and Rand Colton behind the two-way mirror, but turning off the sound that was piped in from the interrogation room to maintain attorney-client privilege.

''I hope he can persuade her to cooperate before she loses all control,'' Thad said, watching as Joe Colton turned away from the glass, his whole posture one of extreme fatigue. ''She's hanging on by a thread, you know. Must be all that practice she's had, impersonating your wife.''

''He'll get her to cooperate, Thad,'' Rand said, putting a hand on Joe's shoulder. ''All of a sudden Silas Pike is singing his lungs out up in Keyhole. He's identified Patsy as the woman who hired him to kill Emily. And then there's Sheriff Toby Atkins. Pike's facing Wyoming's stiffest sentence for killing a police officer, remember? He doesn't have many bargaining chips, and he'd sell his own mother up the river for a chance at serving his time in the most modern facility available.''

Thad nodded. ''Oh, he's singing all right. I got a fax this morning, Rand, one you're not going to like. According to Pike, he was responsible for Nora Hickman's hit-and-run death last year. You know we haven't had any luck solving that one, but Pike knows particulars only the killer would know, so we're pretty sure we've got our man. He says the same woman who hired him to do Emily, hired him to kill Nora, supposedly to shut her up about something. We'll level charges, of course, but it's going to be about two lifetimes before Wyoming is done with him. I'm sorry, Joe. I'm really sorry."

"Poor Nora," Joe said as Rand rubbed his father's back. "She worked for us for years, was a part of the family in many ways. Why would Patsy need to silence her? Nora couldn't have known anything, could she?"

"We'll find out, Dad," Rand told him, looking at Thad. "We'll find it all out, if Jim can get Patsy to agree to an insanity plea in exchange for being committed to a psychiatric hospital. According to Jim, both the district attorney and the judge he spoke to are amenable to a not guilty by reason of insanity plea, if she tells all. She can't testify against Pike if she's judged mentally incompetent, but Wyoming says it doesn't need her, not with Pike spilling his guts faster than the stenographer can type his confession. She goes away, she stays away, and in exchange, as Jim is probably telling her now, we'll keep Joe, Jr. and Teddy, continue to raise them as they're being raised."

"We would have done that anyway," Joe said, glaring at his son. "It sounded like a good idea when I first had it, but not now. I don't like threatening her this way."

"Nobody likes it, Dad, but if we're going to have

answers, and closure, we've got to get Patsy talking, don't we?"

There was a rap on the two-way glass, and they all turned to see Jim Roberts motioning for Thad to reenter the interrogation room. Thad turned up the volume once more, before rejoining the lawyer and activating the video camera.

"It worked," the lawyer told them all in a whisper, standing close to the glass as Thad went through his little time-and-place speech one more time, "and thank God it did, because this woman is highly disturbed. Highly disturbed. I would have pressed for an insanity plea in any case." More loudly, looking at Thad, he said, "My client is willing to plead in exchange for immunity from prosecution and commitment to a psychiatric facility, and will make a complete statement immediately. Can we get a stenographer in here?"

"A mother's love," Joe said in the small, dark room beyond the two-way mirror. "Even sick as she is, we could touch her love for Teddy and Joe, Jr."

"There will still be press, Dad, but it will blow over much more quickly now, as Jim can plead to have everything handled in chambers, without anything said in open court. Pike gets punished, and Patsy is placed in an institution for the criminally insane, most probably for the rest of her life."

"And we get our answers. *All* the answers," Joe said, taking a deep breath, letting it out slowly. "It's enough. It's got to be enough."

* * *

Josh Atkins shifted his body slightly in the saddle and looked across the distance, toward the outbuildings, the red tile roof of the Hacienda de Alegria.

Must be nice, living in a place like this. Safe, protected. Money coming out your ears.

Money to buy safety, to buy silence. Money enough to sweep all the nastiness under a hand-braided rug and forget about it, go on your merry way, get on with your life. Laugh, dance, sing. Eat good food, sleep in a warm bed.

While Toby lay in his cold grave. Forgotten in his cold grave.

Josh tipped back his Stetson, exposing his thick, unruly brown hair, the piercing blue eyes that narrowed toward the rapidly setting sun. His skin was deeply tanned, with sharp lines around his eyes from a lifetime spent squinting into that sun, riding the range in between stints on the rodeo circuit. Slashing lines bracketed his mouth, grown deeper, harder, since the news had come to him about Toby just as he was up for a big ride in Denver.

Josh's body was whipcord lean, taut, and solid muscle. Taller than Toby, older than Toby by four years, definitely less handsome than Toby, whose boyish good looks had mirrored a pure and caring soul.

There was nothing pure or caring or good in Josh's soul as he glared toward the Hacienda de Alegria. There was only hate, a deep and abiding hatred he'd fed with newspaper articles about the grand and glorious Coltons, a hate he nurtured every time he looked at photographs of his brother. His laughing, loving brother who had died because Emily Colton had tricked him into thinking she loved him.

That was how Josh saw it, and he had reason to believe he was right. He had the letters Toby had sent him, letters full of the beautiful Emma Logan, how much Toby admired her, loved her, damn near worshipped her.

Emma Logan. Emily Colton. One and the same woman, the woman who had come to Keyhole, Wyoming, hiding her identity, hiding her reasons for being there.

Josh remembered Toby's first mention of Emma Logan, how he had checked her out in his capacity as sheriff, because her physical description had closely matched that of a female connected to a car-theft ring operating in Keyhole. How Toby had berated himself in the letter that had followed, explaining to his brother that he'd been wrong about Emma, that the beautiful young woman had come to town to try to forget losing her fiancé in a traffic accident, to try to rebuild her life.

Toby had thought he was just the man to help her do exactly that, and Josh had laughed over his brother's letters after that, as Toby had told him of his visits to Emma's cottage, the mega-cups of coffee he drank at the local café where she worked, just so he could be near her. He spoke of her sweet and dimpled smile, her thick mane of long, chestnut-red hair, the graceful way she moved, the softness of her large blue eyes.

Toby had fallen, fallen hard.

And all that time, Emma Logan had been lying to Toby. Emily Colton had been *using* Toby. Using him so that she'd feel safe, knowing that she'd come to Keyhole, not to get on with her life, but to hide from whoever it was she believed was trying to kill her. All of that, and more, Josh had learned from Toby's enraged fellow officers in Keyhole when he'd come from Denver to bury his brother.

If she'd told Toby, alerted him to the danger, then maybe Toby would still be alive.

But she hadn't told him, and Toby had died not knowing why, and probably still believing Emma Logan might have one day loved him. He'd died, alone on the cold floor of a motel cottage, and she hadn't even stuck around to explain. She'd just left him there as he lay bleeding to death, and she'd run, run back to her cushy family and her money and her life.

Bitch. Cold, heartless, conniving bitch.

Josh pulled on the reins, turning his mount, heading back the way he'd come, back to the nearby ranch where he'd taken a temporary job, just so that he could be near the Hacienda de Alegria, just so he could be near Emily Colton. One day meet Emily Colton. One day tell Emily Colton exactly what he thought of her.

Then maybe he could finally learn to deal with his own guilt.

Two

Meredith Colton shivered in her tan wool cape that still carried the cloying, slightly sickening smell of Patsy's dramatic perfume. The perfume was a reminder, as all the clothes in her closet were reminders, that her sister had lived in her house, lived her life, for the past ten years.

She needed to go to town, to shop, to supplement the few items of clothing she'd brought with her from Mississippi. But the furor over Patsy's treachery and Meredith's return to Prosperino had yet to completely dissipate, and Meredith wasn't certain she was strong enough yet to face down the world for the sake of something as mundane as a wardrobe.

So she stuck with her own clothing, was grateful for the pairs of jeans and cotton sweaters her daughter

Sophie had given her, and tried to concentrate on the good things. The many, many good things that had happened since her return to Hacienda de Alegria.

She had grandbabies. Wasn't that amazing? She and Joe were grandparents, several times over. There had been deaths in the time she was gone, but there had also been births, and marriages. The children she had borne, and the children of her heart, had grown, matured, and she was so proud of them all she could just burst.

And Joe. Her dearest, beloved Joe. The man in her dreams, the faceless man who had sustained her, haunted her.

Seeing him again, having him hold her once more, was worth any pain, any sacrifice. Having him near, having his love, had done more to heal her aching heart than anything else.

But nothing could keep her from worrying about Emily, her little Sparrow. It had been Emily who had paid the dearest price, spending years feeling as if her mother had rejected her, having her life threatened. And now, now that it was all over, when Emily should be happy, the child was burdened with the belief that she had cost a good man his life.

Joe said that it probably would be best if Emily never learned that Patsy, in her confession, had told the police she'd ordered the hit-and-run murder of Nora Hickman because she'd overheard Emily and Nora talking about "the two mommies" and worried that Emily had found an ally who might help uncover Patsy's deception.

The records of Patsy's confession were sealed, so Emily would never have to know if no one told her, and Meredith agreed that Emily had enough guilt hanging from her slim shoulders without knowing about Nora.

Yes, Patsy's confession was sealed, and Patsy was, even now, very tightly locked up in an institution for the criminally insane, just as she had been so many years previously, after murdering the father of her firstborn child.

Patsy had been very tightly locked up then, and had gotten out, gotten out to wreak her havoc on the Colton family. Was she locked up tightly enough this time? It was a question Meredith had to ask herself, even as she shivered in the chill, walking through her sad and neglected gardens as twilight fell on a damp, rainy day.

In exchange for telling her story, Joe had agreed to keep Joe, Jr. and Teddy, raise them as his own. They now knew that Joe, Jr. was also Patsy's biological child. They also knew that Patsy had been still actively seeking the infant taken from her at birth so many years ago.

Patsy had fixated on her children, when she hadn't fixated on hurting Meredith, taking her place, stealing her life. And it was her children that had prompted Patsy to cooperate. Joe was even continuing the hunt for Patsy's first child, futile as that might be.

So Patsy was locked up, Meredith was home, and it was time to put the past in the past, get on with the future.

Did Meredith feel safe yet? No. No, she didn't, she couldn't. She had yet to feel quite whole, as there were still some gaps in her memory, and she'd gotten one new shock after another as her family gathered around her—still the same family, yet so different.

Her children weren't children anymore. They had husbands, wives, children of their own. Lives of their own.

And Joe. The years had not been kind to him; Patsy had not been kind to him. Meredith would give her last breath to see the taut lines around his mouth fade into a smile, her hope of heaven to have him lie quietly beside her in sleep, rather than tossing and turning, obviously in the grip of a nightmare.

Time. That was what they needed. Just some time. Wasn't that what Martha Wilkes had told her? Time to heal, time to forgive.

Of all of those hurt by Patsy, Meredith's heart most went out to Joe, Jr. and Teddy. If nothing else, Patsy had been a good if too indulgent mother to her two boys, and they both missed her terribly, were too young to understand that there was a new mommy in their lives now, a new mommy who looked like their old mommy, yet wasn't the same.

When Joe had told Meredith about Joe, Jr. and Teddy, she had wept, partly for the boys, partly for her husband. How he must have suffered when Patsy told him she was pregnant with Teddy, when he knew he couldn't be the father. Yet he had loved "Meredith" enough to forgive her affair, had been man enough to claim Teddy as his own, never knowing that he'd once more been the victim of her sister's deception.

And Joe, Jr. Patsy had admitted that he was hers, the product of a casual liaison with some unknown man. She'd admitted that she'd left Joe, Jr. on the Colton doorstep, knowing he'd be taken in, knowing she planned to join him in a few short weeks. The deviousness of the woman, the near-brilliant manic imagination of the woman.

In exchange for Meredith and Joe continuing to raise the boys as their own and hunting for the baby she had named Jewel, Patsy had talked for hours, for days, outlining her deception, filling in blanks with a sort of fierce pride that just emphasized her mental illness.

She'd tried to poison Joe the night of his sixtieth birthday, had hinted that there had been other plans for other attempts on his life. That had been a shock, a very big shock. She'd laughed as she admitted to being surprised to learn that she wasn't the only one who wished Joe dead, that Emmett Fallon had also been trying to kill the man.

But her most particular glee had come in exposing Joe's brother, Graham, as the father of her son, Teddy. She'd even admitted to blackmailing Graham in order to keep her silence.

Poor Joe. Poor, deluded, betrayed Joe. He hadn't wanted to tell Meredith about Graham, but after one horrible nightmare from which she'd had to wake him, he'd finally blurted it all out. He told her that Rand knew, and he knew, but nobody else knew, and

Meredith urged him to keep silent, for Teddy's sake, at least for now. She didn't know if this was the right or wrong thing to do, whether it was fair to Graham's other children, Jackson and Liza, but she did know that Joe, Jr. and Teddy were Coltons by name, and Portmans by birth. She would raise both boys as if they were her own, and with no regrets.

Meredith stopped in front of the fountain, the one that had haunted her dreams and begun her long road back from the amnesia that had plagued her since the accident Patsy had engineered so many years ago. She put out a hand, catching the cool water as it ran over the rim, listening to the gentle sound of it.

''It's a lot bigger than the fountain back in Mississippi,'' a woman's voice said from somewhere behind her, ''but I think we could have put it together the way we built that one, given enough time and a few margaritas. Hello, Meredith. Your husband thought maybe I ought to visit here for a while, if that's all right with you?''

''Martha!'' Meredith wheeled around to see Dr. Martha Wilkes standing on the patio, shivering in her thin coat not made for a raw November California day. The psychologist was smiling, her dark face lit with humor even as her brown eyes measured Meredith, her patient of five years.

Joe had invited her? What a wonderful man! Just what she needed, to talk with Martha, the one person who understood everything, the one person who wouldn't demand answers because she knew, she knew it all. The one person Meredith could talk to without reserve, without worrying that she might say something hurtful, might have forgotten something important to the other person. The one woman who might be able to help Emily. Meredith's heart swelled with hope.

"Well?" Dr. Wilkes asked with a smile. "It's been a long trip, Meredith. Is that all you're going to say? 'Martha?'"

Meredith launched herself into her friend's arms. "Oh, my God—Martha!"

Emily knew more than her parents thought she knew. She'd gone to Rand when she learned that Patsy Portman had made a full confession, and she'd railed at him, pleaded with him, until she'd learned everything, including the knowledge that her conversation with Nora Hickman had directly led to that good woman's death. Well, Rand hadn't exactly *told* her; she'd guessed most of it. It had been easy to think badly of herself, blame herself for anyone's misfortunes.

She also knew now that Silas Pike had followed her when she'd fled the Hacienda de Alegria, and had found her in Keyhole, helped by Patsy's description of her unique, long chestnut-red hair.

The hair Toby had so admired. The hair that had been her vanity, so that she hadn't cut it, hadn't worn a wig, hadn't disguised herself. She'd been so sure she was safe. She should have cut her hair. Dyed it. Done *something.*

The guilt she felt was crushing, debilitating. And never-ending.

Emily admired her mother's courage, the woman's ability to look for happiness where she could, embrace the family that had not seen through Patsy's deception for ten long years. She was amazed as she watched her mother slide almost effortlessly back into the ebb and flow of daily life at the ranch, her smile always bright even if her eyes were sometimes sad and wistful, her strength of will so obvious to anyone who looked.

Emily envied her mother's courage as well, because she had none of her own. She used to, she was sure of that, but she still had horrifying nightmares about Silas Pike, nightmares where he walked toward her with his curious limping gait, his eyes cold and hard, his Fu-Manchu mustache not quite hiding the leer of his smiling mouth and the large gap between his two front teeth. He walked toward her relentlessly, a gun in his hand, saying, "Well, if it isn't little Emily Blair…or would you rather I call you Emma Logan?"

She felt stripped naked, not just to her real name, but to her fears, the fears that had followed her ever since the night she'd first seen the outline of a man in her bedroom and known that he'd come to kill her.

But that lingering fear was nothing compared to the guilt. Toby had trusted her, Toby had loved her, and yet she hadn't trusted him enough to confide in him, leaving him unprepared to enter her motel cottage and come face-to-face with Silas Pike and his cocked pistol.

So much guilt. Because she hadn't told him. Because she hadn't loved him.

Emily dug the toe of her ancient cowboy boot into the dirt as she stood alongside the corral fence, wishing she could find the shutoff switch to her brain, locate the erase button to the tape that rewound and rewound inside her head, day and night, night and day.

She was supposed to talk to Dr. Wilkes later today, and had promised her mother that she would, but she knew it would be a fruitless exercise. Nobody else could erase that tape for her; she was going to have to live with what she'd done, what she hadn't done.

She was glad Dr. Wilkes could be so helpful to her mother, but her mother had been a victim, and she had no guilt. Emily knew she herself had not been a victim. She'd been proactive all her life, always stating her case firmly if not believably, and then protecting herself as best she could, fighting her own battles.

Right up until the moment Toby Atkins had stepped in to fight her largest battle for her, and died saving her stupid, stubborn life.

Emily turned away from the fence rail, knowing she'd left it too late to take a ride, try to clear her head at least for a little while, and bumped smack into a tall, hard body that blocked her way.

"Emily Colton?" the man asked as she looked up into Toby Atkins's blue eyes.

She blinked, swallowed, stepped back a pace. "Who—who are you?"

"The name's Atkins," he told her, his eyelids narrowing around Toby's blue eyes— No, not Toby's eyes; Toby's eyes smiled. "Josh Atkins. Ring any bells?"

Emily took yet another step backward, her spine colliding with the rail fence. She'd run out of room, had nowhere to run, no place to hide. "Josh...Josh Atkins? Toby's brother?"

No wonder she'd seen Toby in his eyes. But that was all of Toby that could be seen in this lean, hard-eyed man. He wore a huge, sweat-stained Stetson with the front brim folded up on both sides, as if he often rolled the brim between his hands when the hat wasn't shoved down hard on his head. Instead of a sheriff's uniform, like his brother's, he wore heeled cowboy boots, dusty stovepipe-legged jeans that fit like a second skin, a sky-blue cotton shirt and a brown leather vest that skimmed his belt buckle.

If he'd had a six-gun strapped to his thigh, she wouldn't have thought it seemed out of place, as he had the look of a real, old-time cowboy about him, a cowboy about to face off in the middle of a dusty street, guns blazing.

His face was lean, too, darkened by the sun, his nose straight, lines carved into his cheeks and forehead, deep lines radiating from the outside corners of his eyes. His mouth was a wide, unsmiling slash over barely exposed, bright white teeth. A hard yet handsome face. An unforgiving face.

And he hated her, hated the ground she stood on. Nothing could be more obvious.

"How...how did you get in here?" Emily asked when she could find her voice, although she hadn't found much of it because the question came out in a sort of squeak. "The main gates are still guarded."

"Not to a cowboy delivering a mare for stud," he told her, tipping back the curled brim of his hat with one leather-gloved hand. "I'm working at the Rollins ranch a couple of miles from here."

"Oh," Emily said, swallowing hard once again. "I—I didn't know. Toby told me you ride the rodeo circuit."

"I do, but when the season's over I hire myself out to ranchers. Toby probably told you that, too."

Emily nodded, looking away from those hard, hard eyes, that unyielding mouth. "Yes. I think he did. But you worked ranches in Wyoming."

"No reason for me to be in Wyoming anymore, is there, Miss Colton? No reason at all."

Emily pressed both hands to her cheeks. "Oh, God." She sighed, tried to marshal her nerves, dropped her hands to her sides once more. "I should have tried to contact you, shouldn't I? I mean, you have a right to know what happened that night. Toby...Toby saved my life."

"Yeah, so I'm told. And to reward him for that service, you left him bleeding on the floor and took off. Left him alone to die. You have a strange way of saying thank you, Miss Colton. Well, that's enough for now, isn't it? I'll be seeing you again. Again and again. You can sort of consider me your conscience, Miss Colton. Your guilty conscience."

"No!" Emily yelled at his back, for Josh Atkins had turned on his heels and was already climbing into the truck with Rollins Ranch painted on the door of the cab. "No, it wasn't like that! I didn't— Oh, God," she ended, all but collapsing against the fence rails as the truck drove out of the stable yard, toward the main gate. She hugged herself as she watched the truck drive away, tears running down her face. "It wasn't like that...it wasn't like that."

Josh pulled to the side of the road about a mile from the Colton ranch and cut the engine, pounded his gloved fists against the steering wheel.

"Damn," he said once, then twice, then over and over for as long as his breath held out. "Damn, damn, *damn!*"

Well, wasn't he the hero? He ought to get out of the truck, see if he could round up a couple of fuzzy bunnies, then stomp on them. Pull the wings off a few butterflies, drive to town and grab a lollipop out of the mouth of some defenseless baby.

Had he ever seen such hurt in anyone's eyes? Even before he'd said a word, opened his dumb mouth, he'd seen the despair in the way she'd stood at the fence, the defeat in her posture, the weight of the world dragging at her slim shoulders. He'd seen injured animals, plenty of them, and could almost smell them, smell the fear. Emily Colton had been drenched in fear and hopelessness, even before he'd stepped up behind her and made his presence known.

So then he'd kicked her. Hey, she was already down—so why not? She deserved it, didn't she?

"Oh, God," Josh breathed, shaking his head. "I must be losing whatever's left of my mind."

He lay his head back against the headrest, closed his eyes and saw Emily Colton's face. She was just as Toby had described her a million times in his letters. Small, but not too small, with good shoulders for a woman, and straight long legs that looked damn good in jeans.

She'd had on a denim jacket lined with sheepskin, the hem of the jacket just nipping at the top of her small waist, giving her an air of fragility belied by her clothes.

But it was her face that gave away the whole game, even as he'd refused to see what was there. Those sad blue eyes, that flawless yet too-pale skin, the way she sort of hunched her shoulders protectively, as if prepared for life to give her a punishing whack—another whack, because she'd already had a few, hadn't she?

And that hair. God, how Toby had all but waxed poetic about that thick mane of chestnut hair. Toby had once had a chestnut mare just about that same color. He wondered if Toby had made the connection, and doubted it. Emily Colton was one hell of a cut above a rangy old mare that was all Josh could afford to buy his baby brother for his fifteenth birthday.

So, okay. So she was pretty. Beautiful. As beautiful as Toby had said in his letters. And she was hurting. Was she hurting about Toby? Josh wondered....

"It doesn't matter, damn it! She killed him," he

said, sitting up once more, reaching for the key still in the ignition. ''She killed him as much as if she put the bullet in his chest herself. And I'm *not* going to let little Miss Blue Eyes forget that. Not for a very, very long time.''

Three

Meggie James had all the fair-haired beauty of her mother and the never-say-die determination of her father. At the moment, that determination was directed at trying to pull herself up on the coffee table so that she could get her chubby hands on her mother's teacup.

"No way, sweetheart," Sophie Colton James scolded with a smile, redirecting her daughter by holding out a teething ring River's Native American grandmother had fashioned out of thin strips of rawhide.

"Can you believe how much she loves this thing?" Sophie asked Emily, who was holding her own teacup out of the baby's reach. "I've threatened to start calling her Fido, but River just laughs and says his grandmother raised a lot of kids and knows what she's doing. I suppose so,'' she ended, grinning down at Meggie, who had just learned how to lower herself to her plump bottom and was now chewing on the teething ring for all she was worth.

Emily watched as Meggie actually cooed at the rawhide circle, then stuck it in her mouth once more. ''It is ugly, isn't it? I know Mom told me about the thing when Maya's little Marissa was at the ranch the other day, just about gnawing on Mom's shoulder because she's cutting another tooth. In fact, I think Mom said she wishes she'd had a gross of the things when we were growing up,'' Emily said, grinning down at the contented baby who was happily drooling all over her pretty pink coveralls. ''Of course, she also said she'd often thought about keeping us all on stout leashes, but I think she might have been kidding about that one.''

''Mom's great, isn't she? She's back in stride, handing out love and advice, just as if she'd never been...well, never been away,'' Sophie said, lifting her teacup. ''I can't tell you how happy we are that Meggie's finally learned how to get back down once she's pulled herself up. I think Riv and I slept about three minutes all last week, always having to go into her bedroom and lay her back down in her crib. But when I told Mom about it, she said to put the pillows over our heads and let Meggie cry, because eventually she'd let go and figure out that she can get back down all by herself. To hear Mom tell it, we weren't doing

Meggie or ourselves any favors by constantly running to her.''

''Did you let her cry?'' Emily asked, reaching for a homemade cookie Maya's mother, Inez, had baked only that morning and asked her to take with her to Sophie's house.

Sophie winced. ''Not for the first night after Mom's advice. We just couldn't do it. I kept thinking she'd fall, hit her head, all that good stuff you swear you'll never think about, but that you think about all the time once you have babies of your own. But the second night Riv made me watch the clock for ten minutes, and only go to her then—or if we heard a bang,'' she added, shaking her head. ''Seven minutes later, everything was quiet. Riv waited a few minutes more, then sneaked into her room and there she was, sound asleep on her belly, with her rump stuck up in the air. We haven't had a problem since.''

''Moms and grandmothers,'' Emily said, sighing. ''They give good advice, don't they? Or they think they do.''

''Oh, now that sounds ominous,'' Sophie said, picking up Meggie, who had begun rubbing her eyes. ''Let me put this one down for her nap, and I'll be right back. Because being Inez's cookie delivery person wasn't the only reason you rode over here this morning, was it?''

Emily watched as Sophie and Meggie headed for the hallway and stairs, then sat back in her chair, admiring the way her sister had decorated the living room. Part Mission, part antique, somehow Sophie had made it all work beautifully, from the western prints on the walls to the Oriental carpet on the broad-planked floor.

She'd like her own place, her own apartment, but the Hacienda de Alegria was so large that it would be difficult to explain to her mom and dad that she felt cramped, felt the need for her own space. Especially now, with Meredith only back at the ranch for less than two weeks. It had never been right to leave Joe, who had been so unhappy, and it couldn't be right to leave now, with Meredith home again at last.

Still, much as they loved her, Emily was beginning to feel smothered by that love. They watched her, as if she were a fragile vase teetering on the edge of a mantel, ready to fall, smash into a million pieces on the hearth. And now not only were her parents watching her, but Dr. Martha Wilkes was also here, living in the house, eating at the table, being so nice and kind and caring.

The woman was wonderful, really. But Emily felt as if she were constantly under a microscope, so that she was careful to always keep her guard up. Keep smiling, keep helping around the ranch, keep her hurt and despair hidden, locked behind her bedroom door, crying only in the shower, so that no one would hear her. She'd been taking an awful lot of showers lately....

Sophie came back into the room and sat down on the couch with a sigh. "There, that's done. She's been changed and put into jammies, and we'll have blessed peace for about two hours, if we're lucky. Then playtime with Daddy, a bath and dinner—and probably another bath, as Meggie's gotten pretty good at blowing raspberries at us with her mouth full. That's a real treat when she's eating mashed beets, let me tell you. Riv puts her down for the night and sings to her—but you didn't hear that one from me, okay, as he'd probably deny it. He's a wonderful, wonderful father."

Emily looked at her sister, at the smile on Sophie's lovely face, a face still carrying the scar of a mugger's attack. Funny. When Sophie had first run back to the ranch, to hide there, hide her face, it was assumed by everyone that she'd have plastic surgery the moment the surgeon said it was time. But then she'd gotten pregnant, and then there'd been Meggie to take care of, and it was as if Sophie had forgotten the scar even existed. She was too busy living her life, loving her life, to see it.

"You're happy, aren't you, Soph?" Emily asked, knowing the answer. "I mean, you have a sort of *glow* about you."

"Oh, dear," Sophie said, sitting up straight. "It shows? We wanted to wait until Christmas to tell everybody, but if you see it, Mom and Dad are bound to see it."

"See what?" Emily asked, confused.

"That we're pregnant again," Sophie announced, lightly pressing her hands to her flat belly. "We hadn't planned another baby this soon, but now Meggie will have a little brother or sister to play with, and we like that idea. Riv is already planning an addition to the house.''

''That's how Mom and Dad started, isn't it? And the Hacienda de Alegria just grew and grew. I'm so happy for you.'' Emily smiled, while inside she sighed, silently crossing off the idea of coming to live in Sophie's spare room for a few weeks—at least until Dr. Wilkes went back to Mississippi. It had been a bad idea anyway, one born of desperation.

Laughing, Sophie answered, ''True enough, Em, but Riv and I don't have plans to repopulate the entire earth—just our small part of it. Okay, now tell me what's on your mind, and don't tell me 'nothing,' because I won't believe it.''

''I'm that transparent, huh? I thought so, which is one of the reasons I was hoping to come hide out with you guys for a while,'' Emily heard herself admitting, so that she quickly picked up another peanut butter cookie and shoved half of it into her mouth—right next to her foot.

''You want to get away from the ranch? Why?''

Emily pushed a hand through her hair, tucked a heavy lock behind one ear. ''Okay, I'll tell you. Mom's sicced Dr. Wilkes on me, that's why, among other things. The other things I can live with, but Dr. Wilkes gives me the creeps. It's like she can see straight through me.''

''And can she?'' Sophie asked, doing a fair job of looking straight through her sister herself.

''Oh yeah. Straight through me, Soph. It's scary.'' Emily put both hands to the back of her neck, then pushed up, so that her mass of wavy hair all piled high, then fell to her shoulders once more when she moved her hands, making a chestnut cloud around her head. A quick shake of her head and those curls covered half her cheeks and most of her expression. She hadn't even known what she'd done.

But Sophie did.

"Ah, the old hide-my-face-behind-my-hair trick," Sophie said, wagging a finger at Emily. "You do know that's a dead giveaway, don't you, sis? Emily's early-warning system reaction to impending trouble. You've been doing that since you were a kid."

"I have?" Emily went to shake her head, stopped herself. "You're making that up."

"Oh, really? I've got examples, Emily, and I'm more than willing to share. Like the day Mom came into the living room and asked who had broken the glass in a picture frame in the library, and forgotten to take away the baseball that had done the job. That time Dad asked for volunteers to muck out the stalls because half the hands were down with food poisoning. The day the phone rang and it was Mrs. Hatcher, your second grade teacher, calling to talk to Mom. And it wasn't to say that Emily Colton was her prize student."

"Mrs. Hatcher. Ugh! The woman accused me of eating paste. Double ugh! And I'd only taken a small bite."

"Ah, so you do remember. But the point I'm trying to make is that the moment you felt the slightest bit in danger, you found a way to pull your hair over your face, like an ostrich hiding its head in the sand. It was always a dead giveaway. Trouble comes, and Emily hides behind her hair. It's as dependable as Inez's success with peanut butter cookies.''

Emily felt her cheeks flushing, and raised one hand toward her hair before quickly clasping her hands together in her lap. Was her hair always destined to betray her? ''I hate my hair,'' she said quietly, but with a wealth of feeling. ''I should shave it all off.''

''Don't you dare, Emily Colton! You're a beautiful woman, but that hair of yours is absolutely extraordinary. Why, I could pick you out in a crowd of thousands, just from one glimpse of that head of hair. You have enough for five people, all on your one head. And the color! You can't get that out of a bottle, Emily. I know, because I tried one time, in college. I ended up looking like a circus clown.''

''Lots of people could pick me out of a crowd because of this hair of mine,'' Emily said, blinking back sudden tears. ''Oh, damn. Sophie, what am I going to do? Toby Atkins is dead because of me, and his killer told the police that one of the ways he could track me was because of my hair. People remembered it, remembered me, and Silas Pike was able to find me because of it. Toby Atkins *died* because Silas Pike was able to find me.''

Sophie was silent for some moments. ''Oh, wow,'' she breathed at last. ''So you're blaming yourself for Toby Atkins's death? Because of your *hair?*''

Emily shook her head, sniffed back tears. ''No, not really. Not just the hair. But I should have disguised myself, Sophie, or at least cut my hair, hidden my hair. I'm not stupid, I know my hair is distinctive. I'm guilty because I was arrogant, Sophie. I thought I was so smart. I thought I'd hidden myself brilliantly. And then I didn't tell Toby the truth. He was a sheriff, Sophie. I should have trusted him, told him, and then he would have been prepared when trouble came."

"You said all this to Dr. Wilkes?" Sophie leaned forward when Emily remained silent. "Emily? You *did* tell her, didn't you?"

Emily shook her head. "I didn't have to. She knows it was all my fault. Everyone knows," she said, a sudden mental picture of Josh Atkins's hard, condemning eyes making her shiver. She banished that image quickly, knowing it would be back, to haunt her dreams, cloud her days. "That's why she's here, to help me work through my guilt. Like that's going to happen. Like she can somehow change what happened."

Sophie stood up, walked around the coffee table, sat down on the arm of Emily's chair and put her hand on her sister's shoulder. "You do know, Emily, that you're doing again what you said you did about your hair. You're *assuming* that Dr. Wilkes believes you're guilty. I doubt she's as harsh a jury as you've been to yourself. Because I see it another way, sis. I see a young woman running scared from a murderer, running for her life, and yet trying to hang on to as much of her former life as she can. I see a young woman who knew Toby Atkins was falling in love with her, and was too honest to lead him on, make him her protector, put him in danger. You nearly died that night, Emily, and Toby Atkins saved your life. He's a hero, Em. Don't demean his sacrifice. Don't make him into a victim, into your victim. He deserves better than that.''

Emily looked up at her sister, then buried her head against Sophie's side, sobbing.

Josh Atkins felt like a stalker. Probably because that was what he was doing—stalking Emily Blair Colton. His every free hour was spent with his horse tied to a tree as he crouched behind scrub and looked down on the Hacienda de Alegria. He watched the comings and goings at the ranch, waited for Emily Blair Colton to put up her head, sniff the wind and then leave the safety of her well-guarded sanctuary.

Go somewhere where he could get at her, get to her, remind her that he was here, that he wasn't going away.

He'd picked up the Rollins Ranch mare two days ago, and hung around the Hacienda de Alegria until his presence began drawing questioning looks, then had to leave before Emily showed up at the stables. Since then, there'd been no reason, no good excuse, to bring him back to the Colton ranch.

So he'd propped himself against a lamp post on Prosperino's main street, hoping to see Emily Colton come to town to go shopping, to have her hair done, to eat lunch with some friends. That hadn't worked, either. Prosperino wasn't that small a town, but the Coltons were pretty obvious by their absence. Not a single Colton had walked or driven down Prosperino's main street, and Josh could be sure of that, as he had memorized the photographs he'd cut out of newspapers covering the story about Patsy Portman.

Which had brought him back to this hill, this well-concealed vantage point. Another couple of weeks at this, and he'd earn his Stalker merit badge, while losing what was left of his mind.

He might have had no luck in meeting up with Emily, but he had learned a lot about the Coltons, starting with everything he'd read in the newspapers, and added to during his research at the Prosperino Public Library. He might be a cowboy, but he was a community-college-educated cowboy, and he knew how to use the microfiche machine, knew how to go through old newspaper files and find what he wanted.

The Coltons were a good family. He didn't want to admit that, even to himself, but by all accounts they were a good, fine, upstanding family, from Joseph Colton right down to the youngest member.

Hopechest Ranch thrived because of the early interest shown by the Coltons, and all of the family was still heavily involved in the financing of the haven for troubled children, some of them even in the day-to-day running of the facility.

The Coltons had raised their own children even as they'd taken on any number of foster children, even adopted some of them, like Emily Blair Colton. It was one thing for a wealthy, successful man to throw money at a charity, but it was another thing entirely for that man to become so involved, so much a part of the solution.

And it wasn't as if the Coltons always had it easy, been born with silver spoons in their mouths and immune from trouble. Joe Colton had served in the armed forces, then built his empire with his own hands. He'd served his country again as a United States Senator. Joe and Meredith Colton had lost a son to a traffic accident. One of their daughters had almost been killed by a mugger in San Francisco. Joe Colton himself had nearly been murdered by a disgruntled employee.

Not to mention the entire family being duped for ten long years by Meredith Colton's mentally unbalanced twin sister. That had to be the topper.

So maybe the Colton life wasn't a fairy tale complete with the rich and benevolent king and queen and populated by happy, carefree princes and princesses.

But did that excuse Emily Colton from guilt in the death of his only brother? Josh didn't think so. Emily Colton could have run to a dozen different places, put herself under the protection of one of her brothers, or even turned to Joe Colton, who would have surrounded her with armed guards.

Instead, she had run away. She'd run straight to Keyhole, Wyoming, and to Josh's brother, who was just the kind of guy who saw himself as a knight in shining armor, out to put a smile back on the face of the pretty young princess who'd somehow come into his orbit.

"I should have known," Josh muttered under his

breath as he watched the lights coming on inside the sprawling ranch house. "I should have read Toby's letters more carefully, realized he was getting in over his head. I should have left the circuit and gone to Keyhole, checked Emma Logan out for myself."

And he would have, except he'd been chasing another gold buckle, following the rodeo circuit from town to town in Oklahoma and Texas and even New Mexico. Everywhere but Keyhole, Wyoming. Chasing the points, chasing the dream, chasing the buckle of a champion. A grown man acting like a kid, while a kid was wearing the uniform of a sheriff and laying down his life in the line of duty.

Who was the younger Atkins? By age, Toby had been. But by deed, Josh knew himself to be the child, the little boy who'd yet to grow up, take his share of responsibility—that share he'd gratefully dropped after almost single-handedly raising Toby.

It had been *his* turn, or so he'd told himself. He'd been a man when he was supposed to be a boy, and he'd spent the last ten years trying to capture some of the blessed freedom from responsibility most children experienced in their growing-up years.

At least that was his excuse, the one he told himself when he looked at yet another gold buckle, at the prize money he'd spend at least half of as fast as he'd earned it on the back of a bucking bronco.

A few more years, a few more seasons, and he'd settle down, buy himself a small spread with the savings he did have, raise horses and cattle and break broncos to saddle for those who would ride, but not take a chance on breaking their necks to tame a mount.

He would have bought that spread, too, and Toby would have left his sheriff's job in Keyhole and come with him. Josh had planned it all, vaguely, but now that plan seemed as solid as the rock walls of the Grand Canyon, as if he'd only been months away from leaving the circuit. Months away from removing Toby from Keyhole.

Josh took off his Stetson and raked his gloved fingers through his hair. That *was* how it would have been, if Emily Colton hadn't come into Toby's life. It *was.*

Josh had to believe that. He had no other choice. Otherwise, the guilt was all his....

Four

Martha Wilkes sat near the French doors with her hands folded in her lap, looking out onto the patio and Meredith's fountain.

The gardens were fairly bare now, but so well-landscaped that they were still attractive to the eye as the California version of winter approached from the Pacific. It was so peaceful here, so beautiful, and yet the Hacienda de Alegria had been the scene of a ten-year-long nightmare.

Martha had just completed another session with Meredith, although neither of them called them sessions. They just talked. Talked about the house and how Meredith was putting it back to the way it had been before Patsy's rather overblown decorating ideas had changed the casual comfort of the house into something stiff, and formal, and cold.

Meredith's bedroom furniture, which had been stored in one of the outbuildings, was now back in the repainted master suite, as was Joe, who had not slept there for many years. Meredith might not know it, but she was performing a sort of exorcism, banishing her twin sister's presence from this most private sanctuary of her marriage.

"Does it bother you, Meredith, that there was a time when Joe did share that room with Patsy?" Martha had asked over cups of green tea.

"He didn't know," Meredith had replied quietly, then looked Martha square in the eye. "But I'd be lying to you if I didn't think that possibly he *should* have known. Lovemaking...well, it's such an intimate thing, such a unique thing, so special to the two people involved. His wants, my needs, the way we used to laugh and talk long into the night afterward...how could he not have noticed the differences?"

"Is it possible that, at first, he blamed the accident? You supposedly had suffered an injury to your head, remember," Martha remembered suggesting. "And after that, after Teddy? He had his own room from that time on, didn't he? He would have divorced you—Patsy—if it hadn't been for the many years of love that had built your marriage wide and high and deep enough to convince Joe to hang on through the bad times."

"The bad times," Meredith had said, sighing.

"Yes, that's one way of thinking about it all. The worse in our for better or worse."

"Yes, Meredith. Just as you hung on through the bad times you now remember, when Joe was so depressed after your son's death, and again when Joe learned he was sterile. You stuck with him, and in his turn he was, by God, going to stick with you. He loves you, Meredith. He has always loved you. He tolerated that woman in his bedroom, but he never loved her. He loved the memory of *you.*"

Martha closed her eyes, recalling the thoughtful look on Meredith's face when she'd finished speaking. She'd gotten through to Meredith, that had been obvious. But, then, Meredith wanted help, wanted Martha's counsel, was eager to put answers to lingering questions, and then get on with her life. Meredith was anxious to grab at her new happiness with both hands, after a decade spent believing she'd been a murderer, a woman with the most sordid past imaginable. A woman with no family, no love, no real hope.

And if Martha could help Meredith find hope again, feel free to embrace love again, then she would do everything in her power to make it all happen. Because Meredith was more than her patient, she was also her friend.

Martha didn't envy Meredith. That would be ridiculous, considering the hell that woman's life had been, and looking at the struggles that still awaited her these next months, until the patterns of a lifetime overtook and erased the bad years. But she did wish, when she was being Martha, illogical woman, rather than Dr. Wilkes, professional therapist, that she could wake up one morning and find *her* family, *her* children, *her* love of life, *her* hopes for the future.

How had she gone from optimistic girl to this automaton who went through her days, her years, with only her career to show for the trip? No family, few friends. How had she come to be nearly fifty years old, and then wonder where her life had gone? Too late for children. Probably too late for a husband—not that she had ever thought of marrying, even as a young girl. She'd had her career, had longed for her career.

But children? She hadn't realized how empty her arms and heart would feel, at fifty, because of a decision she'd made at twenty.

"Excuse me?"

Martha blinked away her thoughts and turned in her chair, to see yet another slightly familiar face standing behind her. She'd met so many Coltons, biological and adopted and just plain assimilated into this huge, loving family. But she thought she could put a name to this particular face. "Rebecca? Rebecca McGrath? Do I have that right?"

Rebecca smiled as she approached, sat down in the chair placed at a right angle to Martha's. Martha admired the understated grace with which the tall, slim young woman moved, even as her belly swelled with pregnancy. "Yes, Dr. Wilkes, you do. Could I possibly bother you for a few minutes? Professionally."

"Professionally?" Martha carefully slid her psychologist shield up and over her own tender heart, prepared to be friendly, but not make herself vulnerable—or betray any confidences if Rebecca had come to ask questions about Meredith. "Does this have to do with Meredith? I think I recall that you are one of Meredith and Joe's foster children. You work as a teacher for the learning disabled at the Hopechest Ranch now. Am I right?"

"You have a good memory, Dr. Wilkes," Rebecca said, nodding her head. "Especially when I think you must have been introduced to at least thirty of us that first night. And, no, this isn't about Mom, although I do want to tell you how much we all appreciate the way you've helped her over the years. Things could have turned out very differently if Mom hadn't had you to guide her through."

"Your mother is a very strong woman, Rebecca. I don't think there's much that could knock her down for long. Now, how can I help you—if I can help you."

Rebecca pushed her long, brown braid back over her shoulder and leveled her intelligent blue-gray eyes at Martha. "This would be strictly pro bono, Dr. Wilkes, as most everyone who helps at Hopechest does so without payment. I thought I should make that clear up front."

"I do pro bono work, Rebecca. And I'd be happy to help. Is it one of the children?"

Nodding, Rebecca said, "Yes, it is. Tatania. She's seven, and a real sweetheart. Her father is unknown, and her mother died about three months ago, not that the home life was all that great, according to reports from the social worker who'd been assigned to Tatania nearly from birth."

"Drugs? Prostitution?"

"Neglect," Rebecca clarified. "Pure and simple neglect. It happens. Anyway, there was a house fire, which is how her mother died. Tatania was burned, but not too badly, and she came to us two weeks ago. I'm involved because one of the counselors at Hopechest worried that Tatania might be dyslexic, but she's not. She's just too shy and scared to participate in anything—her lessons, interacting with the other children, playtime. Nothing. I think I've heard her say ten words at one go, tops."

"Trauma from the fire? From the loss of her mother? You know, even neglectful mothers are loved by their children. Sometimes more fiercely than you'd imagine. They become little parents themselves, taking care of mommy."

"Anything's possible, I suppose." Rebecca shrugged her shoulders. "I don't know what's going on, Doctor. That's why I'm here. We do have a list of child psychologists, but they're overworked as it is. Plus, Tatania is African American, and I thought... well, that is, I wondered if..."

"If seeing another black face might help?" Martha finished for her, smiling. "Don't be embarrassed, Rebecca. You're right. Tatania might feel more comfortable talking to me. When can I see her?"

Rebecca spread her hands palms up, smiled. "Is anything wrong with right now?"

Martha's professional smile turned into a very real grin. "Not a thing, Rebecca, not a thing. Just let me get my coat."

Emily backed away from the entrance to the living room, feeling like an eavesdropper, and at the same time feeling as if she'd just gotten a call from the governor, giving her a last-minute reprieve.

Dr. Wilkes was going to Hopechest Ranch, and that meant that Emily didn't have to talk to her this afternoon, as she'd promised Sophie. It was the one stroke of good luck she'd had in months, years.

Oh, she'd talk to the woman, eventually. After all, she had promised Sophie she would. But if she could put off that talk for another day, another few days...a week? Yes, that would be good, too.

Emily backed up another few paces, then turned around, smacking straight into Joe Colton. "Um, hi, Dad. Fancy meeting you here."

"Emily," Joe said, looking at her intently. "You wouldn't be hiding from Dr. Wilkes, would you?"

"Who? Me?" Emily bent her head, tugged at the sides of her hair with both hands, so that it fell forward over her face. "No. Of course not. I—I was just heading for the kitchen to tell Inez how much Sophie liked the peanut butter cookies Inez had me take over to her."

"Uh-huh," Joe said, putting his large hand around Emily's elbow and heading toward his study. "Come on, Em, we're going to talk."

Emily bit her bottom lip so that she didn't have a

momentary throwback to her childhood and whine, ''*Must* we?'' and allowed her father to lead her to a leather chair before he went around the desk and sat in his large chair.

This wasn't good. Nice talks took place in the living room, or if in the study, they would both comfortably sit on the large burgundy leather couch. But Joe Colton sitting behind his desk meant they weren't going to talk. They were going to *discuss.*

Joe was the sort of man who would never raise a hand to any of his children, to anyone. But the man could *discuss* a person straight into wanting to dig a hole and then pull it in after her. He just had a way of making you feel so sorry for anything you did wrong, so embarrassed, so upset that you'd disappointed him, that you'd do anything to never have to disappoint him again.

''How are you, Emily?'' Joe said once they were both settled, his gaze loving and yet even more penetrating than Dr. Wilkes's professional gaze by at least one hundredfold. ''Truly.''

''Tr-truly?'' Emily stammered, her mouth dry, her lips stiff. ''Fine. I'm fine. Honest, Dad.''

Joe sat forward, rested his elbows on the top of the desk, his gaze never leaving her face. ''Really. So you've been to town, shopping? Gone to see a movie with friends? Even *talked* to any of your friends? To Liza?''

Emily turned her head away, bit the inside of her cheek. ''Liza's busy in Saratoga, Dad, with Nick and the baby. We've talked, and we e-mail each other, but—''

''Liza tells me you haven't answered any of her e-mails, and that each time she phones you're not available. Liza's a continent away, Emily, and worried sick about you. Don't do this to her.''

Emily mentally hefted a shovel and began digging that hole she wanted to climb into. ''I'm sorry, Dad. It's just—it's just that I'm not really good company right now. Liza would be on a plane in ten seconds, and that's not fair, either. I'll write to her this afternoon. I promise.''

''Uh-huh.''

Okay, the hole was about to get deeper. Joe's last ''Uh-huh'' warned Emily of that. ''There's something else?'' she asked, trying not to wince.

''Yes, Emily, there is. Dr. Wilkes says you've yet to speak with her. She didn't want to tell me, but I guessed. Not that just seeing you do a backward two-step out of the living room wouldn't have given you away in any case. She's here to help, Em. For God's sake, sweetheart, let her help.''

''God helps them who help themselves,'' Emily said with a sad attempt at a smile. ''Isn't that true?''

''In many cases, yes,'' Joe answered, folding his hands on the desktop. ''And in some cases, the best way to help yourself is to *ask* for help. You need to talk to somebody, sweetheart. You can't carry this guilt you're so ready to lug around with you much longer, without really hurting yourself. And your mother is worried about you. There, how's that for guilt? You're upsetting your mother."

Emily sat back in her chair, pushed at her hair with both hands, moving it away from her face even as she longed to hide behind that thick mane. She'd known it coming into the room. Joe Colton never lost, and he had just successfully trumped her ace by bringing her mother's name into their discussion. There was nothing left to do now but admit her defeat gracefully. "Okay, Dad. I'll talk to Dr. Wilkes. I promise."

"Today? When?"

"Mom says you can be just like a bulldog, Dad, grabbing on and refusing to let go. She wasn't kidding, was she? I don't know about today, as Dr. Wilkes was heading over to Hopechest with Rebecca, and I don't know when she'll be back. But soon. Really soon." Then she grabbed at the only straw she could find. "Right after I get back myself."

Joe raised one eyebrow. "Get back? From where?"

Emily rolled her hands in the air, as if trying to conjure up words out of that thin air. "From… from…" She looked up at Joe and smiled as in-spiration finally hit. "From a short camping trip. You know how I love to get out by myself. Just me, my horse, some provisions, and a few nights under the stars. It's always done wonders before, to clear my head."

"It's November, Emily. There won't be any stars. But there could be a lot of rain and wind. No, I don't think that's a good idea."

Neither did Emily, not that she'd admit that to her

father. Camping trips were for the summer months, not rainy November. "Maybe you're right, Dad," she conceded, but reluctantly, because rain or not, just the idea of being on her own—anywhere on her own—was one with an appeal that grew by the second. No Mom and Dad and their worried looks. No phone calls and e-mail from Liza and just about everybody else. No Dr. Wilkes. And no Josh Atkins, showing up right here at the ranch, playing Guilty Conscience. "So I'll think about it, okay?"

Joe put his hands on the arms of his chair, pushed back, and stood. "You're going, right? I've opened my big mouth, stuck my nose in my grown-up daughter's business, and now you're going to take off on your own, just to prove you can do it. I should have kept my mouth shut. Your mother warned me, but I didn't listen. You're just too old to be swayed by one of my famous discussions. Either that, or I'm losing my touch."

Emily stood on tiptoe and kissed her father's cheek as he came around the desk. "Oh, you'll never lose your touch, Dad. Trust me on that one. I was shaking in my boots, coming in here with you. I love you, Dad."

"And your mother and I love you, sweetheart. Remember that when you're camping under those stars. We're here, we'll always be here, and we love you." He gave her a hug. "Oh, and take your cell phone, okay? You don't have to turn it on unless you need to call us, but please take it with you. It may not work in the hills, but it will work everywhere else."

Emily blinked back tears as she smiled, nodded. ''You're the best, Dad,'' she told him, giving him a hug.

''Yes, I am, aren't I?'' he teased back at her. ''Now go pack, and make sure you're out of here tomorrow before your mother finds out. Just leave us both a note, like the trip is a surprise to everyone—and mention that you're taking the cell phone in case you need to contact us. I'm good, sweetheart, but your mother would have my head if she knew I'd agreed to this. Oh, and if you're not back in three days, I'm sending out a helicopter search. Possibly a platoon of Marines.''

''Yes, sir,'' Emily said, saluting, then fairly danced out of the study, feeling suddenly free, really free, for the first time in a very, very long time.

Josh Atkins had just left the post office, where he kept a box, and was heading for the Rollins Ranch pickup truck when he saw a flash of pure chestnut red and stopped cold, hardly believing his luck.

He stepped behind the concealing cab of the brightly painted truck, removing his hat so that Emily Colton wouldn't see him if she looked across the street, and watched as she entered the sporting goods store.

Okay, he could go in there. Anybody could go into a sporting goods store. It wasn't as if she'd walked into a lingerie shop or anything—a place where he'd stick out like a sore thumb.

He unlocked the door to the pickup and tossed his

small stack of mail onto the front seat. There had been three circulars announcing rodeos in towns along the usual circuit, a letter from a woman whose name sounded familiar but whose face had long since escaped his memory, and a good-sized royalty check from that saddle company he'd done print endorsements for ever since he'd been named one of the ten best all-around riders three years earlier.

Locking the door, he took a deep breath, let it out slowly, and headed across the street. Pulling open the door to the store, he tipped the brim of his Stetson a few fractions lower over his eyes and stepped inside.

Big store. Bigger on the inside than it had looked on the outside. He bypassed the baseball and football equipment, skirted a rack of bowling balls and made his way toward the rear, where he saw glass cases full of rifles. He veered left when he realized that he couldn't quite see Emily Colton toting a hunting rifle.

That took him to the rather large camping supplies section of the store…and to Emily Colton.

He stepped behind a towering display of camp stoves and listened as she spoke with a sales clerk. "I can't believe I put my sleeping bag away wet, Janice. I was taught much better than that," she was saying as the clerk grinned and pointed toward a shelf stuffed with sleeping bags. "Talk about *moldy!* Still, it was at least ten years old, and I'll bet there are much warmer and more sophisticated ones now."

Janice, the sales clerk, said something Josh couldn't hear, and then Emily, who was closer to him, though her back was turned, said, "Oh, just two or three days. I know it might rain, but I'll chance it. I'm riding out into the hills tomorrow morning, if you've got a good sleeping bag for me, one that rolls up small enough to tie on the back of Molly's saddle. Oh, this one is great! Velcro *and* zippers? Janice, you're a genius. By tomorrow night it will be just Molly, me, and the stars—and the fried chicken I've asked Inez to make for me, of course.''

Josh slipped silently into the next aisle, turning his head and pretending a great interest in automatic hot socks.

She was riding out into the hills? Tomorrow morning? Just her and Molly, some fried chicken—and him?

Oh, yes. Definitely him.

Sometimes the gods did smile.

Five

The morning dawned gray, but warm. Emily decided to take that as a good sign, but she still turned on the radio to catch the daily forecast. There was a storm forming over the Pacific, but the weathercaster cheerily declared that he'd "bet my sweet bippy" that the threatened storm would head south, missing the Prosperino area.

That was good enough for Emily.

Inez was banging pots in the kitchen when Emily came through, lugging her sleeping bag, her carefully—even skillfully—packed backpack slung over her shoulders.

"There's enough food here for two days, if you don't make a pig of yourself the first day," Inez said, handing over a canvas sack that Emily planned to hang from the horn of her Western saddle. "Where's your coat?"

"Hanging on a peg down at the stables," Emily reminded the woman, "which is exactly where you said I had to keep it, because it always smells like horse."

Inez pulled a face. "Your slicker?" she asked, obviously on a hunt to find something that Emily had forgotten, just so she could say, "See? What would you Coltons do without me?"

"With my coat."

"Uh-huh. Plastic sheeting to put under your sleeping bag?"

"Got it. Got it, got a flashlight—with fresh batteries. Got my first-aid kit, got three extra pairs of socks and my heaviest boots, got a paperback book to read, got my handy-dandy automatic fire starter. Okay?"

"Your cell phone," Inez said, pointing a finger at Emily. "Your father told me to remind you about your cell phone."

"Damn," Emily said in exaggerated disgust. "You've done it again, Inez. I completely forgot the cell phone." She hadn't, but if it made Inez feel better, what was the harm in a little white lie?

"And it's all charged and ready to go?"

Now Emily's grimace turned real. She slipped the backpack from her shoulders and unzipped one of the outside pockets, withdrawing the cell phone. When she turned it on, the battery indicator showed it to be working at only half power. "Well, I'll charge it."

"Where, Missy? You going to plug it into Molly? I don't think she'd like that. Here," Inez said, pulling a silver-faced cell phone from her pocket. "Your father told me to give this to you. Now, if you're going, I'd say you'd better get yourself gone. You know your mother gets up early, and neither of us wants to see her blocking the door, her arms stretched out to keep you from leaving."

"That wouldn't be a pretty sight, would it?"

"No, which is why I'm standing here, trying not to do it myself. There could be a storm, you know."

"Weather Willie says it's going to miss us, go south." Emily gave Inez a swift kiss on the cheek, then slipped her backpack over her shoulders once more. "I need this, Inez. I really, really need this."

"I know," Inez said, quickly turning her face so that Emily couldn't see her expression—although she had thought she'd seen the quick glint of tears in the woman's eyes. "So you go have a long conversation with the wind and the hills, and get yourself rid of whatever's banging around inside that pretty head of yours. We'd like to see our Emily Sunshine smile again, you know, all of us."

Emily blinked back quick tears of her own, nodded, slammed her worn Stetson on her riot of chestnut curls and headed toward the stables.

Josh looked up at the darkening sky, and wondered if Emily Colton had taken a moment to look back over her shoulder, at the thick clouds rolling in from the ocean.

Probably not. The woman had set a leisurely pace, and kept to it for the past two hours, heading almost straight east, then slightly north, toward the hills in the distance. She hadn't stopped, she hadn't looked back, she hadn't done anything but ride. Like a woman in a trance.

Not smart. Not smart at all. A lone rider had to be constantly alert, on the lookout for danger, be it under her mount's hooves, or behind her, high in the sky—or riding another horse, following her, carefully keeping his distance, yet always keeping her in sight.

He'd say one thing for her, the woman could sit a horse. Her back ramrod straight, she sat the saddle easily, gracefully, as if born to ride. Like the cowboys of old, she could probably keep up her pace, and her fine seat, for hours and hours and hours.

So she wasn't a tenderfoot, or worse, an idiot. That was good, because Josh really didn't feel in the mood to ride to the rescue of a damsel in distress.

What he did plan to do, however, was still pretty nebulous. He'd already figured that he'd keep out of sight when she stopped for a meal, because she'd still be too close to the ranch and could simply mount her horse and ride away from him.

He'd wait until dark, which came early in November, and for her to stop for the night. Once she was settled, and too far from the ranch to risk her mount with night travel under a moonless, starless sky, he'd ride into her camp and make himself known.

Unless she was heading toward some cabin? Possibly toward friends who lived out here, pretty much in the middle of nowhere?

No. He doubted that. She'd bought a sleeping bag, hadn't she?

Yes, the woman was on her own, and chances like this didn't come along twice. He'd follow, wait, bide his time, and then he'd ride in, confront her, and make her admit her guilt in Toby's death.

He just wished he didn't feel so much like a heel.

Joe Colton placed the phone back on the receiver and dropped his head into his hands. Would it stop? Would it ever stop?

"Joe?"

He looked up, to see Meredith walking into his study. Quickly, he rose from his chair and went around the desk to take her in his arms. He couldn't seem to touch her enough, hold her enough. "Hi, babe," he said, kissing her hair. "You about ready for lunch? I think I smell Inez's special chicken soup. Good day for it, with the weather being so raw."

Meredith gently pushed herself away from her husband, leaving her hands resting on his upper arms. "Emily's gone, Joe. She rode out this morning on one of her solitary jaunts. I found a note from her in her room. She expects to be gone at least three days." She tipped her head slightly, looked up at her husband. "And you knew."

Joe took Meredith's hand and led her over to the couch. "Yes, I knew," he admitted, sighing. "I tried to talk her out of it, but she was adamant. She feels overwhelmed right now, by us, by Martha. Too many eyes, watching her, even if we're trying to help her.

The hills are her bolt hole, Meredith, and always were. So, yes, I let her go.''

''She mentioned that she's taken her cell phone,'' Meredith said, folding her hands in her lap. ''That's how I knew you were in on the plan, in case you're wondering. That sort of careful preparation has you written all over it.''

Joe smiled sheepishly. ''Sometimes your memory is *too* good, sweetheart.''

Meredith gave him a small smile. ''Well, you have to admit it, darling. Not everyone packs an extra toothbrush and a first-aid kit to go on his honeymoon.''

''I'll never live that one down, will I? And I told you, that stuff was just left in the suitcase, and I forgot to take it out.''

''Of course it was. Right next to three new pairs of pajamas, still with the sales tags on them.''

Joe put his arm around her shoulders, pulled her close. ''Those tags never did come off, did they? Because the pajamas never made it out of the suitcase. Now *there's* a memory I'm glad you didn't forget. Or maybe not. Maybe I'd like to refresh your memory.''

He kissed her then, and Meredith returned the kiss, raising a hand to stroke his cheek. But then she pulled away and stared deeply into his eyes. ''Nice try, darling, and I'll be sure to take you up on it later. However, I got the feeling when I walked in that something's wrong, something's upset you. I heard the phone ring a few minutes ago. Is there bad news?''

Joe took her hands in his. ''Yeah,'' he said, squeezing her fingers. ''I was going to tell you, but not until

I had an update from the doctor. Meredith, Patsy tried to kill herself this morning."

Meredith closed her eyes. "Oh, dear God." She gripped Joe's hands, hard, and looked at him. "Is she all right? Did the doctor say she's all right?"

Nodding, Joe said, "They got to her in time. No one knows where she got the knife—a homemade affair—but the doctor told me they're always finding weapons the inmates, uh, the patients, have fashioned out of odds and ends. She slit one wrist, not too deeply, although there was a lot of blood, and Patsy tried to hold off the attendants with the knife when they came to help her. The doctor thinks it wasn't a serious attempt, more of a cry for help, but they've got her in the infirmary on a suicide watch."

"A cry for help? What sort of help? I want to see her," Meredith said, her lips tight. "Make the arrangements, Joe. I don't want to hear that it's impossible. Do what you have to do, call whoever you have to call. I want to see my sister, Joe. *Today.*"

It wasn't until two o'clock that Emily finally realized she was hungry. She had snacked on a granola bar earlier, when she'd stopped to water Molly, but her stomach had been just about the last thing on her mind.

She'd been too busy remembering. Remembering the many times she'd ridden this same countryside, gone off on her own to commune with nature—as her father had called it—to be alone, to dream her dreams. How innocent she had been, even as she'd lived with the damning thought that something was very wrong with her mother. Living with the frightening, mind-blowing thought that the woman was not her mother at all.

Emily drew Molly to a stop at one of her usual resting spots next to a small, fast-running stream and dismounted. Tying Molly's reins to a branch on a nearby tree, she left the horse to graze in the long grass, then lifted the canvas bag from the saddle horn and sat down on her favorite large rock that jutted out over the stream.

Fried chicken. Definitely the fried chicken. She rummaged in the insulated bag, taking out a small see-through container holding a leg and a wing—her favorites—and unwrapped the clear plastic wrap holding some celery and carrot sticks. She'd eat, then refill her canteen from the stream, and be on her way, already knowing that she'd have plenty of time to reach the cave before it got too dark.

She looked to the sky, just to double-check the time she'd glimpsed on her watch, and frowned as she saw the line of black clouds over the coastline. Damn. She hadn't been paying attention—and Weather Willie just lost the bet on his sweet bippy. There was going to be a storm, and it wasn't going to slip to the south.

Why hadn't she been paying attention? Unless she hadn't wanted to look back, to think about the possibility of a storm, because that would have meant she would have to postpone her camping trip.

She took one longing look at the chicken, stuck one crispy chicken leg between her teeth, and refilled her half-empty canteen from the stream. Tucking everything else back into the bag, she then untied Molly and mounted her with the ease of long practice, using the rock as her step up.

Once in the saddle, Emily looked toward the dark clouds again, and then toward the hills. Could she make it? She lifted her head, sniffed the air, at last becoming aware of the increase in the wind, all of it blowing in off the ocean.

If she turned back toward the ranch, she'd be riding straight into the storm. If she rode toward the cave, the sanctuary she'd always kept stored with dry wood for a fire, and which held her camp stove and other supplies in a large plastic container she'd dragged up there two summers ago, she might be able to outrun the storm.

Definitely the cave was the lesser of two evils. Besides, the last thing Emily wanted to do was go back to the ranch. Not yet. She gave a flick of the reins, heading Molly toward the hills.

She didn't look back, because looking back wouldn't help her. The storm was coming. That was all she had to know.

If she had looked back, she might have caught a glimpse of Josh Atkins, remounting his own horse, ready to follow her wherever she led.

Because Emily was right. The storm was right behind her.

Martha watched as Meredith slid her arms into a full-length raincoat Joe held out to her. ''Are you two sure you want to do this? Patsy is highly disturbed, and she hates you both. This could get nasty. Perhaps you should wait, give it a few days, then speak with the doctor again?''

''I can't do that, Martha,'' Meredith told her. ''Joe told me the doctor said Patsy's suicide attempt was a cry for help. Hate me or not, I'm all she's got. She has to have directed that cry to me.''

''Then let me come with you,'' Martha suggested, reaching for her own coat. ''She may need to see you, but she doesn't need to see Joe. I'm sorry, Joe, but just the sight of you might set her off. I'm sure I can convince her doctors to let me accompany Meredith into Patsy's hospital room.''

Joe looked at Meredith, who nodded her agreement, and within minutes they were in the car and on their way. Forty minutes later, with the windshield wipers losing their battle with the windblown rain, they arrived at the gates of St. James Clinic, a part of the state's institution for the criminally insane.

Martha watched Meredith closely from the back seat as Joe drove through the gates, for Meredith had once resided here, after the engineered automobile accident had robbed her of her memory. Patsy had brought her here, to these grounds, and left her, unconscious, where the staff would find her, recognize her as Patsy and lock her up in a mental institution.

The amnesia, or as the doctors at St. James had termed it, her ''disassociative fugue,'' had only been a bonus to Patsy, who had believed that only Meredith's insistence that she was *not* Patsy would be enough to keep her sister locked up for years and years.

"Are you all right?" Martha asked as she and Meredith exited the car in front of an imposing pair of doors cut into the dark brick building and stepped under the overhang, out of the worst of the weather.

"Yes, I'm fine," Meredith said as Joe went to her, gripped her hand tightly in his.

"Maybe so," he said, trying for some sort of gallows humor perhaps, "but I'd still like to put a name tag on you, just so these guys remember who you are—and who you aren't."

"They were very kind to me in the short time I was here, before I went to Mississippi," Meredith said quietly. "I can only hope they're being as kind to Patsy."

Meredith need not have worried, for once inside the large foyer they were greeted by a young doctor who immediately took her and Martha upstairs to the infirmary. "I've bent a few rules here, Mrs. Colton, but this is a pretty extraordinary case. Dr. Wilkes? It's nice to meet you. According to everything I've read in the newspapers—and I admit to following this story with great interest—you were a major factor in returning Mrs. Colton to her family."

"Thank you," Martha said, her sharp brown eyes seeing the institution for what it was, a prison with few amenities for the criminally insane. The paint on the walls was dull, the windows all barred, and the general atmosphere was as gray and chilly as this November day. "It looks like you have the same budget woes as we do in Mississippi, Doctor," she said as an attendant unlocked the last of a set of three secured doors leading to the infirmary.

"Budget cuts are the bane of my life," the doctor agreed with a wry smile. "Still, we do what we can. Do you mind? I have to stay with you, as does Dave, our attendant."

Meredith stepped through the doorway without answering, and the doctor, Dave and Martha followed her. The room they entered was long and narrow, with equally narrow beds lining both walls. Surprisingly, other than the last one on the left, the beds were empty. But in that last bed lay Patsy Portman, her head turned away from the doorway, her wrists and ankles in cloth restraints, her left wrist heavily bandaged.

"Go slow," Martha warned Meredith, taking her arm for a moment. "Just say hello, and see where Patsy wants to go from there."

Martha followed close behind Meredith, then stopped some ten feet from the bed as Patsy turned toward them, the fire in her eyes looking like Hollywood special effects. Martha felt a shiver trace icy fingers down her spine as she looked into the face of Patsy Portman—a face stripped bare by insanity, turned ugly even in its patrician beauty.

"Well, well, well, look who's here," Patsy said, her grin grotesque, drool running from one corner of her mouth. Antipsychotic drugs, Martha decided. They often had side effects that included drooling, twitching, and sometimes even a blank expression that could appear almost masklike. Patsy wore that mask now, but it didn't expand to include those hot, searching eyes.

"Patsy," Meredith said, reaching out a hand, then drawing it back. "Are you...are you all right?"

Patsy's grin widened. "Oh, yeah, I'm great. This afternoon we're having a pool party. Last night it was a first-run movie in the assembly room, and tomorrow we're having Queen Elizabeth to tea. Am I all right? God, Meredith, you were always such an *idiot!*"

The doctor stepped forward, but Martha held out an arm, silently motioning for him to stay where he was, say nothing.

"Yes, you always were the smart one, weren't you, Patsy?" Meredith said, her tone surprising Martha, because it sounded so much like her own professional tone. She guessed that Meredith hadn't been in therapy for five long years without learning a few tricks of the trade. "Always prettier, too, Patsy. Everyone said so."

Patsy's smile turned Cheshire-like, and the woman actually looked as if she were about to preen, to purr. "And everyone was right, too," she crowed, even going so far as to toss a come-hither wink at Dave, the strapping attendant. Then, just as suddenly as that mood had hit, it disappeared, to be replaced by Patsy's trembling bottom lip, and even a tear. "Merry, you've got to help me. You're the only one who can help me."

"That's why I'm here, Patsy. I was told you needed

my help.'' Meredith looked to Martha, who nodded, and then she stepped closer to the bed. ''We're taking care of Joe, Jr. and Teddy, Patsy. We always will.''

''I know. I could hate you more if you weren't so damned *good.* But it isn't enough. I'm never going to get out of here, Merry. Not this time. So you have to help me. Before my mind goes, before these damn drugs they're forcing on me make me forget. You have to find my Jewel.''

''Your— What do you mean, Patsy?''

''Jewel! Not a what. A *who.* My daughter, Merry. The one that bastard Ellis Mayfair stole from me. That was my only mistake, you know,'' she went on, the cunning look back in her eyes. ''I shouldn't have killed him until he told me where he'd taken her. I've looked, Merry. I've spent a fortune, looking for her. She's out there, I know it.''

''And you named her Jewel?'' Meredith asked, stepping even closer, placing her hand in her sister's. ''But that was so long ago, Patsy. If whoever you hired couldn't find her in all this time—''

Patsy's knuckles turned white as she gripped Meredith's hand, so that Dave stepped forward, ready to assist. ''Idiots! I hired idiots! You and Joe have more money than God, Merry. You can find her. You *have* to find her. I'll give you a month, Merry. A month, or next time I'll slice deeper. I mean it, Merry, I'll slice clear through to the bone.'' Her lips drew back over her teeth. ''You slice lengthwise, Meredith, *down* the arm to open the artery, not across the wrist.

I know how. I know how, and I'll do it. These idiots can't stop me."

Dave pried Patsy's fingers loose and Martha turned Meredith by touching her shoulders, then led her out of the room.

"Does she mean it, Martha?" Meredith asked as they rode the elevator back to the lobby. "Will she really kill herself next time?"

"It doesn't matter what I believe, Meredith," Martha told her quietly. "It's what you believe, and what you can live with."

Meredith gave an abrupt shake of her head. "We're going to find her, Martha. We're going to find Patsy's daughter. I don't know how, but we're going to do it. We have to!"

Six

Emily had pulled her rain poncho from her backpack when the wind picked up, even though the sound of the thin plastic, slapped hard by that wind, always set Molly to dancing, her ears flicking as she objected to the strange noise.

She pulled up the hood overtop her Stetson as the wind got worse, coming at her from the rear, nearly pushing her forward in the saddle. The sky was getting darker, too soon to be losing the light, and as she neared her hill—her private hill—the branches of the trees around her whipped in the air. The long grass was bent nearly sideways, and one small, dead branch had come flying past her, heavily catching her on the left shoulder.

Then the rain came. Slashing, stinging, cold as hell.

The sky lit with lightning, boomed with thunder, and a near waterfall kept running off the brim of her Stetson, then blowing into her eyes. She could barely see, barely navigate, and she put most of her faith in Molly's surefooted judgment and the mare's memory of their destination.

For the last one hundred or more yards of the way, Emily had to dismount, lead Molly uphill through the scrub and rocks, beneath the blowing trees. But the cave was up there, large enough for both her and Molly, dark and damp, but blessedly dry and out of the wind and rain.

She slipped off her backpack and grabbed the flashlight from the outside ring that held it at the ready, the strong light cutting through the teeming rain as she searched out the well-hidden mouth of the cave.

There. There it was. The opening was nearly obscured by the growth of grass, and almost blocked by a freshly fallen limb. "Damn," Emily muttered, wondering how she'd get Molly over that branch and into the cave.

She braced the flashlight against a small rock, aiming the light toward the cave entrance. "Where's a good forklift when you need one?" she asked herself, already reaching for the coiled rope on her saddle, planning to tie one end around the branch, the other around Molly's saddle horn. She might not be able to move the heavy limb, but Molly could.

Emily's fingers were stiff inside her leather gloves, icy cold and clumsy as she tried to tie the rope around the heaviest part of the limb. Then the sky lit, bright as noon, and the heavens broke in two with a crack of thunder that shook the hillside.

"Molly, no!"

Emily dropped the length of rope and ran toward her mount, who was already badly spooked, her eyes rolling in her head. Before Emily could reach her, there was another blinding flash of light, another clap of thunder, and Molly reared, wheeled and took off down the hillside.

Emily watched the mare run off, taking with her the sleeping bag, the food, the water, and even the backpack Emily had shrugged out of, hanging it around the saddle horn by one strap. The flashlight had also come to grief, and lay smashed where Molly's hoof had crushed it. Gone, everything was gone, either broken or heading back down the hill on Molly's back, and Emily was very much alone on the hillside with nothing but the clothes she stood up in and the stupid length of rope.

The rain, which had already been falling in earnest, doubled in intensity so that, Emily knew, a sheep standing out in such a downpour, and stupid enough to look up, would drown—or so she'd been told. Emily did lift her head to take one look at the black sky, but quickly lowered it again. She was dumb to be out here, but she wasn't as dumb as a sheep!

Clawing her way, Emily half stepped, half crawled over the sharp branches of the limb, and left the rain behind her as she all but fell onto the floor of the cave.

So dark. She had to crawl, feel her way, until at

last her fingers touched the plastic container holding her camp stove. Her handy-dandy automatic fire starter was in her backpack, but she was sure she'd left a box of kitchen matches in the container. Please God, let her have matches.

Teeth chattering, fingers stiff with cold, she flipped open the lid of the container, grateful she'd not seen the use of putting a lock on plastic, which could be cut open by anyone who really, really wanted to see what was inside. Not that *she* could have cut it open, because her knife was in her backpack and her backpack was heading downhill on Molly, but then being grateful for small favors was, it seemed, going to be all she had right now.

It took minutes, felt like hours, for Emily to pull out the small camp stove, rummage in the bottom of the container and find the box of kitchen matches that would light the propane in the portable tank. Once it was lit, she could use the flame to ignite some small bits of dry shrub, then light the wood fire she always left ready to go before she broke camp.

She might be hungry, she might be on foot, stranded until the storm was past her, but at least she could be dry and warm.

So much for Josh's tracking skills. The woman was gone, lost in the artificial night and rain so fierce that his vision was limited to only a few feet in front of him.

He should have followed her more closely, shortened the gap between them before she turned her horse into that thick stand of trees at the base of the hill. But he hadn't, and now she was gone, out of sight, and he was slowly drowning as he sat his horse, wondering where to go next, what to do.

And then he heard it. Off to his right. A noise. A crashing. The sound of an animal in pain.

He guided his horse toward the noise, now a screaming that sickened him in his gut. His own mount tossed its head, absorbing the panic of that raw scream, and Josh had to fight to keep his seat as he relentlessly moved toward something he didn't want to see.

Dismounting, he firmly tied his mount's reins to a stout branch and proceeded on foot, toward the barely discernible shape of a fully-loaded horse down and flailing.

The woman. Where was the woman? Where was Emily Colton?

Don't let her be under the horse.

Josh circled the mare, gingerly reaching for the dragging reins, all the while talking, trying to soothe the panicked mass of bone and muscle and razor-sharp hooves. All the while, he scanned the scene as best he could, looking for Emily Colton, not finding her.

He dragged his full attention to the horse. All four legs were flailing, and obviously not broken. That was one small favor. In fact, it would appear that the horse was more frightened than injured, and that the heavy load on its back was giving it most of its trouble—

rather like a turtle flipped onto its shell and powerless to right itself.

But more than the weight was holding the mare down. Sure enough, there was a backpack dangling from the saddle horn, the second strap caught up in a branch that now bent all the way to the ground.

"They make these things stronger every year, almost stronger than steel. Must be those new space-age materials I keep reading about. Yeah, well, snared like a rabbit in a trap, weren't you, girl?" Josh said, removing the backpack from the saddle horn, then giving Molly a solid *whomp* on her hindquarters so that she struggled to her feet. The mare would have run off again, but Josh had a firm hand on the reins, and a basically gentle saddle horse was no match against his skills. Within moments, Molly was standing quite still, looking rather embarrassed that she had caused such a fuss.

"Where's your lady, girl?" Josh asked the horse, stroking the mare's white-blazed face. "Where did you leave her?"

Maybe Dr. Dolittle could talk to the animals, and there was that book about a guy who whispered to horses, but Josh knew he'd pretty much struck out when Molly dipped her head and began chewing on some damp grass close against the base of a nearby tree.

He'd have to find Emily Colton on his own, and dragging two horses with him while he was at it, because only an idiot would try to move, mounted, through these dense trees.

The woman was more trouble than she was worth, and seemingly born to get into trouble, into scrapes she needed to be bailed out of by some dumb sucker who believed it his duty to help damsels in distress. That was how Toby had gotten involved with Emily Colton, and now here he was, next in line to audition for the role of knight errant.

Man, talk about having a bad feeling about something; Josh sensed danger in this whole, mixed-up situation. Danger to Emily Colton, who was out in the middle of nowhere without her horse or supplies, and danger to himself, who for some ungodly reason actually felt worried about her.

Josh returned to his own mount, untied him and led him back to Molly, then looked uphill as if some sort of divine intervention would show him where Emily and Molly had parted company. Was the woman lying hurt somewhere? Broken leg? Broken neck?

And then he saw it. Through the dark and the lashing rain, he saw it: smoke.

Lifting his head, he sniffed the air like a hound ready to go on point. Yes, definitely wood smoke. Yet it was raining, all the wood from here to the Pacific was wet, too wet to burn. How the hell…?

"Come on, kids, let's check this out," he said to the horses, urging them forward, one lead in each hand, his shoulders straining as the animals made known their reluctance to climb the hill.

His boots slipping on the wet ground, Josh kept moving forward, moving straight up the hill, seeing the path Molly had made in her panicked descent whenever helpful lightning flashed, momentarily illuminating his way.

The smell of wood smoke got stronger, and Josh's stomach growled as if the smell of a campfire equaled the aroma of meat cooking on a spit hanging over that fire. He was cold, he was wet, his boots weren't made for hill-climbing, and Josh's temper was riding a razor edge as he moved on, sure his shoulders would be pulled from their sockets as the horses reacted to the next crash of thunder.

Lightning flashed, and Josh tensed for the boom that would surely follow, but in that moment of illumination he saw a length of whitish rope lying on the ground, one end tied to the base of a thick, leafy branch.

"What the—?" He stopped, and when the wind whipped around, it sent an even stronger whiff of wood smoke to his nostrils. Squinting, he could swear the smoke was coming from behind the tree limb, coming straight out of the hillside.

A slow smile crept over his face, and he tied Molly to a tree branch, then led his own mount forward. What a woman could start, a man nearly always had to finish. He tied the loose end of the rope to his horse's saddle horn, and then walked the animal backward, so that the tree limb, heavy with rain, began to slowly inch away from what he was sure would be the mouth of a cave.

Emily was feeling pretty proud of herself, even as she worried about Molly. But the storm would be over in the morning, and Molly would either return to the cave on her own, or Emily would find her somewhere on the hillside. She believed that because she needed to believe that, and since she couldn't change anything, she did her best to pretend that everything was all right, would be all right.

Molly wouldn't go back to the ranch on her own, Emily was at least sure of that. No, she'd stick around, waiting for Emily to find her, and then look ashamed as she tried to root in Emily's pocket for a carrot.

Which wouldn't be there, because Emily had already eaten it.

Emily had also stripped herself to the skin, getting out of all her wet clothing once she'd gotten the fire started, laying her clothing on rocks near the fire after she'd wrapped herself in the old wool army blanket she kept in the container.

For the past ten minutes, now that her teeth had stopped chattering, she'd sat on a smooth rock beside the fire, enjoying her dinner. Cans of ravioli, a hand can-opener and her camp stove had transformed the small cave into a five-star restaurant, even if Emily had barely waited for the ravioli to be warm before hungrily spooning it into her mouth.

She was just raising the spoon to her mouth one last time, to lick it, when the tree branch at the mouth of the cave began to move.

Earthquake?

No, that couldn't be. Everything would be moving if it was an earthquake.

The tree limb kept moving, opening the mouth of the cave to the wind and rain, and letting the wood smoke more naturally find its way out into the night, even as Emily moved more deeply into the cave.

She held the blanket close to her as she looked longingly at her clothing for a second or two, then watched the mouth of the cave, knowing a bear wouldn't have moved the branch, and wondering what could be out there that was as strong, and as dangerous, as a bear.

Why didn't she have her rifle? Why had Molly run off with the thing tucked into a leather scabbard on the saddle? Why had she been so dumb as to come up here, into the hills, in the first place?

Nothing happened for the next few seconds. The branch was gone, and the night was quiet, even the thunder ceasing long enough for Emily to be able to hear her own heart rapidly beating in her ears.

And then she saw a hat, a Stetson. The hat was attached to a tall, black slicker-clad male-type body that walked into the cave on cowboy-booted feet. She couldn't see the face, but she recognized the boots. Stupid thing, to recognize a pair of boots, but these were a sort of beigy snakeskin, and very distinctive. She even remembered that Toby had told her his brother had won the boots in one of his rodeos.

She felt very naked under the blanket, which she was, but she also was mad. Madder than hell. The man had followed her! There was no other answer, no other explanation.

God, would she have to take the next space shuttle

in order to get away from people, away from this one most intimidating person?

"Evenin', ma'am," Josh Atkins said once he was standing on the other side of the fire, looking straight at her. He pushed the hood of his slicker from his head, then touched the brim of his drenched Stetson as if bidding her good day.

"Go away," Emily said, wincing as the power of her frantic voice echoed inside the cave. "Just...just go away."

"Be the gentleman, you mean?" Josh asked, taking another step in her direction. "You're asking the wrong man, Miss Colton, if it's a gentleman you're looking for tonight. Besides, I've got two horses out there, and they need to come inside. It'll be cramped, but we can do it."

"Two horses?" Emily spoke in spite of herself, hope flaring that Josh Atkins had found her Molly. "Are they both yours?"

"Only if I was into horse thieving, which I'm not. I found your mare down near the base of the hill. What happened? Did she throw you? Or are you dumb enough to leave a horse's leads trailing in the middle of a storm? Horses aren't dogs, Miss Colton. They don't sit or stay on command."

"And just when I thought I was going to have to thank you for finding my horse," Emily said, one corner of her mouth definitely trying to slide into a sneer. "Well, don't just stand there—get them in here."

"Used to giving orders, are you?" Josh tipped his

hat back on his head, his harshly handsome features clearly shown in the light from the fire. "Funny, but that's not how it works out on the range. Each man takes care of his own horse."

Emily tried to hug the blanket even closer. "I—I can't. I…I'm not…"

"Yes, I had noticed that," Josh drawled, his gaze going to the shirt and jeans and underclothes spread out to dry near the fire. "In that case, we'll make a trade. I bring in your horse, and you open another can of that ravioli I must have been smelling even half-way down the hill. Deal?"

Mutely, Emily nodded. "And then you'll leave?"

She watched as Josh tipped back his chin and laughed, a clearly amused yet rather sarcastic sound that put her teeth on edge. "Leave? Miss Colton, there's the mother of all storms going on out there, in case you didn't notice. It'll probably go on for days. Leave? I'm not going anywhere. Neither of us is going anywhere. Which is pretty handy, because you and I have a few things to talk about, don't we?"

Emily actually felt the blood draining from her face, even as her body grew hot. "I have nothing to say to you that you'd listen to, Mr. Atkins. You've already drawn your own conclusions, not that I care what you think."

"You care what *everybody* thinks, Emily Colton, or you wouldn't have been riding up here to hide with a storm coming in. So let's not kid ourselves, lady. I'm here to tell you about my brother, to let you know just how much you destroyed when you let him walk blindly into that death trap. And then, if you have the guts, the gall, you can tell me why you did it, try to make me understand.''

Emily blinked back tears even as she bit back a sharp reply. She just looked at him levelly and said, ''The horses won't get any drier standing outside, Mr. Atkins.''

He returned her stare for a few moments, then replaced his Stetson, lifted up the hood of his slicker, turned on his heel and headed out of the cave.

''Oh, God,'' Emily groaned, sinking to her knees. She had nowhere to go, nowhere else to run. She was here, and Josh Atkins was here, and neither of them were going anywhere until the storm passed. Days. He said it might be days. How could she possibly survive in this cave with him for *days?* And nights...

Emily got to her feet, quickly gathered up her still-damp clothing and ran to the back of the cave, out of the light, to get dressed.

Meredith stood at the French doors, her arms folded tight over her chest, and watched the rain that lashed across the patio. She heard footsteps behind her and asked, without turning around, ''Did you hear the latest weather report, Joe? Is there any sign of this letting up?''

His large hands touched her shoulders, began kneading the tightness out of them, and she relaxed as much as she could, leaning back against his strength. ''No change, sweetheart. This storm is going to hang on for another day and night, and then a second storm could come in from offshore. Or it could miss us entirely, go south.''

''In other words, they don't know,'' Meredith said, sighing. ''Why do they say it *might* go here, or it *might* go there? Why don't they just admit it—they have no idea what the weather is going to do. All their computers, all their science, and my grandmother Portman's bunion was a better indicator.''

Joe bent and kissed the side of her throat. ''That's it, sweetheart, take out your anger and frustration on the weatherman. He probably deserves it.''

Meredith turned in his arms, smiled up at him. ''I know I'm being silly, Joe. Did you make that call?''

''To Austin? Yes, I caught him just as he was heading to his father's house for the weekend. Peter's fine, by the way, as are all the McGraths. Anyway, Austin said he'd postpone his trip and stop by here tomorrow, to get as much background information from us as he can.''

''It's difficult to believe that the Austin I remember as a child has had such a full and sometimes tragic life. But I'm really amazed that he's actually a private investigator, and that he was so much help to you when Emmett...''

''When Emmett tried to kill me,'' Joe finished for her, leading her over to one of the overstuffed couches. ''Austin was a great help to us all, Meredith, and when he and Rebecca fell in love, well, I wish you had been here to see the way she blossomed, began to glow.''

''I'm just glad they're here now, that Austin agreed

to move here from Portland so that Rebecca could stay near us. So, he's coming here tomorrow?''

''Eight o'clock,'' Joe confirmed, nodding. ''Rand has faxed me copies of a lot of information that was found in Patsy's papers, although what they do is just pretty much rule out a lot of leads. No, don't frown, sweetheart. If this Jewel is out there, Austin will find her.''

Meredith smiled wanly, shaking her head. ''I can't seem to get rid of my memory of the way Patsy sounded as we left her. She means it, Joe. She will kill herself. And let's face it, she's never getting out of that institution. With us taking care of her boys, the only thing keeping her going is the chance to maybe see her Jewel again. I can't help wondering, Joe, if she'd never gotten pregnant, if that man hadn't sold away her baby only hours after her birth...well, maybe Patsy wouldn't be so sick and none of these past ten years would have happened.''

She looked down at her hands that twisted in her lap. ''And if I had told you I even had a twin sister...''

''Don't,'' Joe said, gathering her into his arms. ''Patsy wanted you to leave her alone. She even faked her own death so that you'd leave her alone. We can't look back, see how things might have been different if we'd acted differently. They happened, sweetheart, and now we're together again. I don't want to waste a moment of our new time together, thinking about the heartache of the past.''

Meredith lay her head on Joe's shoulder and looked

toward the French doors, toward the lightning that flashed in the night. ‘‘It’s what we want for Emily, isn’t it?’’ she asked quietly. ‘‘That she put the heartache of the past behind her and get on with her life. Her timing could have been better, but I guess she really needed to be alone, to think things out before she speaks with Martha. Do you really think she’s safe out there?’’

‘‘Safe and dry, sweetheart,’’ Joe said confidently. ‘‘Our Emily’s had a lot of experience in taking care of herself, being on her own. She’ll be fine.’’

Seven

It was while unsaddling Molly that Emily saw the gash. ''She's cut,'' she said, automatically turning to Josh Atkins, a man—she had just silently sworn to herself—she wouldn't speak to even if her hair caught on fire and he was the only one within fifty miles with a canteen of water.

But this was different. This wasn't about her, this was about Molly.

Josh deposited his mount's saddle near the fire, obviously planning to use it as a pillow, and walked over to look where Emily was pointing.

''She was so wet, I didn't notice at first, but this is blood,'' Emily said, her stomach twisting into a knot as she withdrew her hand, looked at the blood on her fingertips. She bent closer to the mare's neck, trying to see the severity of the cut. "God. Do you think it needs stitching?"

"Hard to say," Josh told her, then took a folded blue-and-white handkerchief from his pocket and pressed it against the wound. "First we clean her up, then we decide."

"It's my fault," Emily said, her bottom lip trembling. "I never should have listened to Weather Willie."

The makeshift compress held tight against Molly's neck, Josh turned to look at Emily. "You want to run that one by me one more time? I don't think I understand."

"Weather Willie," Emily said, clumsily wiping her hands on her jeans, then dragging the backs of her hands across her cheeks, to rid them of the tears that had escaped her stinging, rapidly blinking eyes. "I listened to the radio this morning, and Weather Willie promised that the storm would go south of us, would miss us. He's never right, and I know it. I just wanted out of there so badly."

"Yeah, you are pretty lousy at running, not that it seems to have stopped you. And damn if each time you run somebody else doesn't go and get hurt," Josh said, and Emily's shoulders tensed, as if preparing to ward off a blow. "Here, take a look at this," he then said, obviously not caring whether or not his last words had offended her, hurt her. "It's not that bad a cut, although she does have several scrapes, doesn't she? Probably ran too close to a tree, and probably when she lost that sack of food you were telling me about—all that fried chicken we aren't going to get to eat. I've got some antiseptic in my saddlebags. That ought to fix her up."

"Don't bother," Emily replied stiffly. "I have my own first-aid kit. I'll take care of her. I'd phone down to the ranch, for help, but the phone's broken. Molly must have rolled on it. Yeah, well, you just go make up your bed, so that I know where to make up my own—which will be as far from yours as I can get it."

"I don't think so," Josh told her, shaking his head. "Or maybe you haven't noticed. It's raining out there, Miss Colton, and in here, that fire of yours is dying for lack of fuel. Unless you've got another stash of dry wood, I think we're going to have to be a lot closer together than you're planning on, if we want to get through the night without hypothermia. In case you were wondering if yet another Atkins was willing to die for you. Because this one isn't, even if staying alive means also keeping you alive."

Emily looked at him, looked over at the fire, and then turned her back, picked up her backpack and stomped to the other end of the cave. Once there, in the semidark, and feeling safer, she said, "You have a sleeping bag strapped to your saddle, and mine is guaranteed for temperatures a lot colder than we're having tonight. I'll be fine."

"Good for you," Josh said, unrolling the sleeping bag tied to the back of his saddle, then using it to cover his mount's bare back. He then picked up the heavy wool army blanket Emily had been using earlier and draped that over Molly's back. "Now, guess who has the only sleeping bag left? Unless you don't care what happens to these horses?"

"I don't care what happens to *you,*" Emily said, knowing she was being ridiculous, petty, spiteful. She took in a deep breath, let it out slowly. "Isn't there any other way?"

"Sure," Josh said, efficiently arranging the remaining articles—Emily's rifle, his own saddlebags—then picking up Emily's saddle and placing it next to his. "In the old days, men used to kill their horses, gut them, then slip inside their bellies to get out of the wind and snow. Supposedly, the warm bodies kept them safe for hours."

Emily's eyes narrowed as she glared at Josh across the dying fire. "Was that really necessary? Did you have to tell me that? No, don't answer me, of course you did. I do really hate you, Mr. Atkins," she said, turning off the propane in order to save fuel.

They'd need that camp stove again tomorrow, and for more than heat, and she knew it. Josh knew it. Josh knew the fire was going out. Josh knew the only way they could both stay warm was to crawl into that sleeping bag together. Josh knew too damn much!

"What are you doing now?" she asked as he gathered up his flannel-lined slicker, and her own thin plastic poncho.

"We need to keep as much of the weather outside as we can, although we can't block the whole entrance, not with the fire still going." He reached for the length of rope he'd untied, recoiled, after moving the branch. "Here, give me a hand with this."

After several false starts, Josh somehow managed to secure the ends of the rope across the mouth of the cave, tying them to stout bushes at either side of the entrance. He was drenched to the skin by then, once he was done, but the rope finally held taut and tight. When he hung the slicker and poncho over it, like clothes drying on a line in a suburban backyard, the opening of the cave was covered by at least half.

"That should hold," he said, heading for his saddle bags, rain dripping off his long brown hair that now lay plastered to his well-shaped head.

He pulled out a length of toweling and rubbed at his wet head, then smoothed his hair back with both hands. Emily involuntarily inhaled a quick breath as she watched as he then stripped off his vest and shirt, so that he was bare to the waist, his tanned, sleekly muscled skin glowing in the firelight. She saw a long, whitish scar on his side, another riding high on his chest, probably trophies from the rodeo ring. "Wh-what do you think you're doing?"

"Trying not to freeze to death," he said, pulling a clean, plaid flannel shirt from his saddlebag. "The jeans have got to go, too, so unless you're into free shows, I suggest you turn your back."

He hadn't finished speaking before Emily did just that, her face burning even as it was turned away from the fire. She could hear him pulling off his cowboy boots, and listened as he grunted a few times, probably having to wrestle with the tight, wet jeans in order to remove them. Then the slap of heavy denim being unfolded and shaken and, at last, the sound of a zipper being zipped.

Emily exhaled, not realizing until then that she'd been holding her breath. She turned and looked at him as he sat down on the saddle, began pulling on warm woolen socks before reaching for his boots.

"All done, and you didn't peek. Good for you, Miss Colton. Now, if you give me a minute to pull on these boots, I can turn around so I can do you the same favor. Unless you plan to sleep in those damp clothes?"

Did she trust him? Perhaps more to the point, did she really want to climb into her sleeping bag while wearing jeans damp at the hips, nearly dripping wet at the hems? No, she didn't. Not really.

Glaring at him, she unzipped her backpack and pulled out her only change of clothes, a flannel shirt in a plaid closely resembling the one he wore, and a pair of jeans. She withdrew two pair of woolen socks and some fresh underwear, which she first rolled into a ball inside the backpack and then hid inside her folded shirt before he could see them.

The last thing she needed was for Josh Atkins to learn that she'd brought along tiger-patterned bikini underpants and a matching underwire bra.

"Turn around, please, Mr. Atkins," she ordered, tipping up her chin.

Josh's smile was rather like Toby's, except not quite so innocent. "For a quarter," he said, holding out his hand. "One of those from the Denver mint, with the states printed on the back. I still need Pennsylvania to complete my set.''

''Go to hell,'' she said, heading for the darkest part of the cave. She undressed quickly, trying to stay as ''dressed'' as possible even as she stripped, pulled on dry clothes. All the while, she had one eye trained on Josh Atkins, making sure his back stayed turned.

''You may now resume your customary sarcastic stance,'' Emily gritted out, knowing she was being petty.

''You're welcome,'' Josh answered brightly, and Emily shivered, her nerves bristling. There was no dealing with this man. None.

She peeked at her slim gold wristwatch as she walked back toward the fire, skirting the now cold camp stove, the plastic container and her unzipped backpack. The cave was large, but getting more claustrophobic by the minute. She hesitated, stopped and then laid out her damp clothes over the container, before stuffing her discarded underwear in a zippered compartment of her backpack.

She unzipped another compartment, bringing out her wide-toothed comb and a fabric-covered elastic band, plus her folding toothbrush and travel-size tube of toothpaste. A small burgundy hand towel, a squeeze tube of liquid soap, and she was ready for her nighttime rituals. She might be in the wilderness, but there were certain amenities of civilization she would never abandon.

Surprisingly, she saw that Josh was holding his own toothbrush as she joined him at the fire. ''I didn't know cowboys paid much attention to the National Dental Association recommendations,'' she said, reaching for her cup of water that she'd left on the ground.

''What's the matter, Miss Colton? Too domestic for you? Don't worry, I won't be asking for a kiss good night...or anything else.''

There was nothing to say to follow up such a statement, so Emily chose not to answer, possibly prolong this uncomfortable conversation. She just sat down on her favorite flat rock, turned her back and brushed her teeth, the sound of the brush seemingly echoing off the walls of the cave. She rinsed her mouth with water from the cup, but couldn't bring herself to spit it out on the ground, so she swallowed it. He was right. This was all just too domestic, too intimate...too unnerving.

She kept her back to him as she combed her hair, dry now, and a riot of tangled curls. She didn't know that those curls shone brightly in the firelight, that her head looked topped by fire itself—warm, touchable fire that flowed down onto her shoulders.

''I'll...check on the horses,'' Josh said from behind her, his voice sounding a little strained. Or maybe, Emily thought, it was the sound of the storm raging outside that had put this edge in his voice.

''Okay,'' Emily said, pulling back her hair, ruthlessly securing it in a ponytail at the base of her hairline. ''I don't know about you, but I'm exhausted, even if it is only nine o'clock. Besides, I'm hungry and we can't eat anything else if we want the food to last, and I'm getting cold again and want to get inside the sleeping bag.''

''Yeah,'' Josh said. ''We can do an inventory of your food and mine in the morning, combine what we've got. Oh, and about the sleeping bag? I see that you've got a ground sheet, and so do I. That'll keep us dry, but it won't do much to hold off the cold of the ground in here, because sunless caves don't exactly collect any heat during the day. Doubling them up will help some, but since we can't both fit inside your sleeping bag, we're going to have to unzip it completely and use it as a blanket for the both of us. It's our shared body heat that's going to keep us from hypothermia. But you've already figured that out, right?''

Emily watched as Josh went over to the horses, adjusting their blankets, making sure their leads were well-secured beneath the rocks he'd used to keep them at least superficially tied. He checked the bandage on Molly, obviously satisfied with what he'd seen.

He was so tall, his shoulders so broad, even as she could see that his upper body was in the shape of a T, narrowing to a flat stomach and tight waist, a compact backside and long legs hugged by his tight jeans.

He was all whipcord muscle and easy grace. When he walked, in those boots of his, his entire body moved with each long stride, carrying his energy with him, his confidence swinging along with his arms. He was the Marlboro man without the dangerous cigarettes, the rugged, solitary hero on the cover of a

Louis L'Amour novel, the secret dream of every silly teenage girl who'd ever been to the rodeo.

And he was going to be sleeping next to her tonight, sharing his body heat with her tonight.

Would sleep ever claim her?

Would morning come soon enough?

Would she wake in his arms, turning toward his heat during the night?

If she did, what then?

"He hates you, remember?" Emily muttered under her breath, and then reached for the folded ground cloth, knowing she would have to make the bed she would lie in. "And you're not all that cracked up about him."

Josh stayed with the horses longer than necessary, fussing over them, checking each of their hooves, quietly talking to them as the storm kept them both skittish. Then he went to the front of the cave, inspecting the makeshift windbreak, looking out into the night sky, watching the rain that showed no sign of letting up.

They could be here for at least one more day and night, as the hillside was rapidly turning into a mud bath that would make it nearly impossible for the horses to safely get down to flat country.

Could he do this for another day and night? Hell, could he make it through this one night?

He hadn't counted on being in Emily Colton's company for more than a few hours. He'd wanted to talk to her, tell her about Toby, make her see how gravely she'd injured his brother, injured him.

And, yes, he'd wanted to hear her side of the story. He figured he owed her that much, if only because Toby had loved her. Maybe there had been some sort of extenuating circumstance, some reason she'd run away, left Toby to die alone. If there was, he needed to hear it.

He especially needed to hear it now, now that he'd felt himself dangerously sliding into that same trap Toby had embraced so eagerly. A trap laid by a riot of chestnut curls, a pair of large, innocent blue eyes and a matched set of dimples in her sweetly beautiful face.

She was no china doll, not the least bit fragile-looking. Her build was fairly athletic, with good shoulders and narrow hips. Dolly Parton wouldn't have to worry about any competition in the bust-size department, and yet…and yet there was just something about the way she moved that was so entirely female, so enticing….

Josh shook his head, shook himself back to reality. He was here because this woman had caused the death of his brother. Not deliberately, but caused it just the same. By the sin of omission, the sin of not being straight with Toby, not telling him who she was, why she was hiding in Keyhole—not telling him that she might be bringing danger to Keyhole.

And she'd left him. She'd let him rescue her, take a bullet for her, and then she'd left him.

Josh wasn't about to forget that.

Having run out of chores, and his resolve back in place, Josh returned to the campfire to see Emily trying to arrange the opened sleeping bag over the layered ground sheets.

"Here, let me help you," he said, grabbing onto the sleeping bag and spreading it carefully. "Nice material. Light, and yet probably warmer than it looks."

"It's new," Emily said avoiding his eyes as she gave the material a two-handed pat, as if making sure it wouldn't move, fly away. "Right or left?"

Josh hadn't been paying attention. "Pardon me?"

"I said, right or left?" Emily repeated. "I sleep on my right side, so I'd like to be on the right, if that's okay with you?"

He also slept on his right side, and had a quick mental image of the two of them sleeping, spoon-like, his belly to her back, his arm snug around her waist, their legs entangled underneath the covers.

"Left," he said, longing to clear his throat, which had suddenly gone tight—almost as tight as his jeans. He dropped his hands, clasped them together in front of himself, hoping the dark of the cave would do the rest. "I'll take the left side. But we'll have to lose one of the saddles, share one, or else we'll be too far apart. Body heat, remember?"

"We'll try it first my way, which means you on your side, and me on mine," Emily told him stiffly, even as she crawled across the sleeping bag, her bent head nearly colliding with his knees. She pulled back the cover, slid beneath it, her head resting on the seat of the saddle. "Man," she said, moving about, clearly trying to get comfortable, "I haven't done this in a long time."

"Slept with a man?" Josh winced, his mouth moving way too much faster than his brain.

"I've never—" Emily covered her face with both hands for a moment, then angrily yanked the covers up and over her shoulders. "I haven't slept here in the cave for a long time. Get your mind out of the gutter, please, Mr. Atkins. Your *brother* was a gentleman."

"Yeah," Josh grumbled, stepping over Emily's body and sitting down on his saddle, ready to remove his boots. Damn, the woman was a virgin. How the hell had that happened? Was the whole male world blind? Doggedly, he kept insulting her. "He sure was a gentleman. And look where that got him."

Emily remained silent, which was probably a good thing, and Josh tossed his boots to one side, then slid his long body under the sleeping bag.

He lay on his back, looking up at the dark roof of the cave, one arm bent behind his head as he wished himself anywhere but where he was at this moment. The dying fire cast strange, moving shadows against the craggy roof, and an ever-changing wind often blew smoke back into the cave, to hang high against the rock.

Ghost riders in the sky. Josh could see them up there, shades of old cowboys, riding their ghostly horses through eternity. Was that his destiny? Without Toby around to settle him, ground him, would he spend the rest of his life following the rodeo circuit, taking odd jobs in the off-season, growing old and tough and doing it all alone?

What else was out there for him? A home, a family? Toby had been his family—did he really want another? Could he survive losing another? Losing Toby had damn near destroyed him.

Josh turned his head to the right, unable to see the color of Emily's hair in the darkness, but able to discern the outline of her slim body beneath the sleeping bag. Emily Colton had a family. A large family. Where had that gotten her?

She couldn't take too much comfort from them, or she wouldn't be here, hiding away in a cave rather than staying safe and warm with her loved ones. Hell, her loved ones had damn near gotten her killed.

Maybe there was something to say for his solitary life, a life without entanglements.

So he'd end up with arthritic knees and a bad back. He'd wear his scars, and his injuries, and he'd soon spend more time in bars tossing back beers and reminiscing about the good old days than he would in the ring. The rodeo was a mistress, a tough mistress, a demanding mistress.

Maybe he'd been following that mistress for too long. If he'd only broken away sooner, turned his back, Toby might be alive now...and he wouldn't be here, in a damp cave, trying to keep his mind and hands off the woman who'd helped kill him.

Josh held his breath, listening in the dark for the sound of Emily Colton's breathing. The horses whinnied and blew softly, the fire crackled as it burned down and the wind continued to howl. Thunder rolled off in the distance.

And yet, through it all, he swore he could hear, not Emily Colton's breathing, but the chattering of her teeth. Not that she'd say anything, not that she'd complain.

Stubborn woman.

Idiot man. Idiot because he worried, idiot because he cared. He sat up, pushed his saddle out of the way, then lifted the covers up and over his shoulder as he turned on his right side.

He moved closer, until he felt the stiffness of her rigidly held body, then lay down, his head mashed uncomfortably on the high-rising back ridge of her saddle. It didn't matter. Being uncomfortable didn't matter. Because he'd never sleep tonight, not with the heat of Emily Colton's body burning into him, not with his arm wrapped around her thin waist, his fingers itching to touch what lay higher—her smooth stomach, the rise of her breasts.

He couldn't remember ever passing a whole night with a woman in his bed. He certainly knew he'd never spent the night with a virgin.

Eight

"Grandma's going to be so happy to see your new braces, Sparrow," Meredith said, smiling into the rearview mirror at Emily, who did not smile back.

"I'm not going to show her," Emily said, barely opening her lips to speak. "I'm not going to show anyone. Sophie called me Metal Mouth. And Amber said how now I could get in radio stations all the way from San Francisco. She said I was one big antenna head."

"Sisters. They tease," Meredith said on a sigh. "And remember, both Sophie and Amber had braces, and their brothers teased them. It's a family tradition, handed down from child to child, and just shows how much they love you."

"Well, I don't like them much right now, and I hate

these braces. They hurt and I can't chew gum and Inez wouldn't let me have corn on the cob last night. She sliced it all off the cob. It doesn't taste as good that way.''

''It's true, sweetheart, there are sacrifices to be made. But just remember that soon your teeth will be all nice and straight and that prettiest smile in the whole world will be even prettier.'' Meredith took another peek in the rearview mirror. ''Emily, push your seat belt lower over your belly, okay? It shouldn't be riding so high on your waist, in case we have an accident.''

Emily did as she was told then, because she was in a bad mood anyway, groused, ''I don't see why I can't sit up front with you. I haven't sat in the back seat since I was a baby.''

''The seat belt up here is broken, Sparrow, and we're going to get it fixed tomorrow. In the meantime, pretend you're the lady of the manor, and I'm your chauffeur, okay?''

Emily brightened at that. ''Does that mean I can give you orders?''

''Your wish, madam, is my command.''

Giggling, Emily folded her arms over her belly, tipped back her head and commanded: ''To the ice cream parlor, my good man, and step on it!''

''What about your grandmother?''

''Oh, yeah. Well, we'll pick her up on the way. Grandma likes ice cream, too.''

''Yes, ma'am, anything you say, ma'am,'' Meredith agreed, tipping an imaginary hat to her ''employer''

in the back seat, and Emily laughed, her smile wide, her braces forgotten.

A tune Emily particularly liked came on the radio and she asked Meredith to turn up the volume. They both began to sing along, Emily laughing when Meredith stumbled over a few of the words.

Happy. They were so happy. And then Meredith looked in the rearview mirror again, probably to see Emily's smiling face, and her hands tightened on the steering wheel.

"Now why is that car following us so closely? The road's deserted except for the two of us, and it's a passing zone. Oh, just go around me if you're in such a hurry," Meredith said, addressing the occupant of the following car as if the driver could hear her.

Emily turned in her seat, trying to look out the rear window, but the seat belt restricted her movement. She sat forward once more, feeling the power of the car as Meredith stepped on the gas.

"Sit front, Emily, and hold on. There's barely any shoulder here in front of the ditch. I'm going to pull off up ahead, where there's a rest zone, and let this idiot driver by. He's so close I can't even see his grill."

Emily did as she was told, reacting to her mother's calm yet deadly serious tone, closing her eyes as the scenery whipped by, the interior of the car quiet because Meredith had pushed the button that turned off the radio.

And then it happened. A bump. A bump from the rear. Once. Twice.

"Hey!" Emily yelled, angry, but more frightened than anything else. "Hey—cut it out! Mom, make him cut it out!"

But Meredith didn't answer except to say, "Cover your face with your hands, Sparrow! Protect your face!" because a third bump, harder than the others, had sent the car onto the small shoulder of the road, the right rear tire blowing as it dropped down from macadam to gravel. Meredith struggled to regain control, but couldn't get the two right wheels back up on the macadam.

They kept going, but now they were going sideways, sliding, heading hood-first into the ditch…then stopping all of a sudden, so that Emily's body was shoved forward, roughly pulled back by her shoulder harness. Her head was jarred to the right as the car tipped onto its side, and she hit the side window, and everything went black…

"Mommy…" Emily blinked, and just blinking made her head hurt so badly. "Mommy…"

She opened her eyes again, fighting the pain, and looked toward the front seat. There was her mommy, still sitting in the driver's seat, her forehead bleeding.

No. There was her mommy, pulling open the drivers' side door, leaning in, looking at Emily.

Two mommies?

Oh, her head hurt. Emily's head really, really hurt. "Mommy, something's wrong with me. I can't see right. Mommy, my head hurts. And my belly's sick. I'm going to be sick."

"Shut up, you whiny little brat!"

Emily looked at her mother, at both of her mothers, and began to cry. One of the mommies had yelled at her. Shocked—in shock—Emily watched as one of the mommies opened the back door and crawled in beside her.

"Here, drink this. It will make you feel better."

"Don't want...don't want..."

Emily felt her head go back as her mommy pulled hard on her hair, and the next thing she knew she was choking on a horrible-tasting liquid...which was also the last thing she knew until she woke up in the hospital, hours later, to see one of the mommies looking down at her in the bed.

"Which mommy are you?" she asked, her mouth dry, her head aching.

The mommy looking down at her just smiled....

"No! You're not the right one, you're not the right one! Where's my mommy? What did you do with my real mommy? Mommy? Mom! Mom!"

"Wake up, Emily. Come on. You're having a dream. Just a dream. Wake up for me, wake up now."

Emily opened her eyes and looked straight into the piercing blue eyes of Josh Atkins as he hovered just above her. His shaggy hair fell forward over his forehead, and he had a heavy, golden-brown stubble on his cheeks. His mere closeness made her pulse leap, her mouth go dry.

Emily's heart still pounded hurtfully in her chest, but she was coming awake now, the nightmare was fading. She wasn't in the hospital. She wasn't eleven years old. She was in her cave. She was lying down, and Josh Atkins, who hated her, was leaning over her, his body pressed close to hers.

"Get off me!" she ordered, pushing at his shoulders with both hands. "Just get your big, stupid self *off* me!"

He stayed where he was. "Not exactly a morning person, are you?" he asked, then slowly withdrew, to lie down beside her as she shivered at the withdrawal of his body heat. "Want to tell me about it? That must have been one hell of a dream."

Emily would have gotten up, except that she was already chilled, and the fire was out, and it was still raining outside the mouth of the cave, the dawn gray, forbidding. "No-o-o, I don't want to tell you about it. I'm too busy wishing you on the other side of the world."

"Nice. Real polite of you," Josh said, pulling his saddle forward from where he'd pushed it last night and settling himself against it, half lying, half sitting. "You were calling for your mother. Your *real* mother. I'm not a rocket scientist, but I have read all the newspaper stories that have been out there lately. You were in the car, weren't you, the day Meredith Colton's sister ran her into a ditch, then changed places with her? How'd she do that anyway? The papers were sort of vague. I mean, that St. James place was more than a half hour's distance away from the crash site. How did she get Mrs. Colton there, and then get back to the car where you were? Didn't anyone pass by? Didn't anybody stop?"

Emily's hands closed into fists at her side. She

didn't want to talk about this, just wanted to forget it. Yes, her questions had been answered, all of them, but the dreams, instead of fading, had only become more clear. Used to be, she couldn't remember Patsy climbing into the back seat, couldn't remember having medicine poured down her throat. That memory had come back after Patsy's confession. Maybe that was why the dreams wouldn't go away. Maybe she had to live through the whole thing, just one time, before she could tuck her memories away, lock them behind a closed door in her mind.

She pushed herself up a little, dragging part of the sleeping bag with her as she leaned against her saddle. She should be telling Martha Wilkes what she remembered now, not Josh Atkins. Still, the nightmare was so vivid, still scaring her, and if she didn't tell someone, anyone, soon, it would probably haunt her all day.

"She drugged me, then somehow got both Mom and me into her own car. She tied a white handkerchief around the antenna of Mom's car, so that it just looked like a disabled vehicle, abandoned and awaiting towing, which is why nobody stopped. Who stops to look inside an empty car?"

"Smart, I suppose. Then what?"

Emily pushed a hand through her hair, then tugged at the band holding it, pulling it off, then shaking her head so that her curls tumbled around her shoulders. She raised a hand to pull the curls forward, to cover her cheeks, hide her expression...then stopped. Sophie had made her too aware of her "ostrich" mannerism for Emily to take any comfort in it anymore.

"Patsy—that's my mom's sister—said she drugged Mom, then put her out of the car on the St. James grounds, where the authorities would find her, recognize her as Patsy because Patsy had once been an inmate—patient—there, and treat her. Lock her up. Which they did. And with Mom having amnesia? Well, it certainly didn't help Mom, but it sure helped her sister."

"And you?"

"I don't remember, of course, but Patsy explained that she went back to the scene—the whole thing must have taken about two hours—parked her car down the road, put a white handkerchief on *that* antenna, then carried me back to Mom's car. Actually, she didn't make it back to the car before someone came along to help her, but she just acted all dazed and confused, saying she'd been in an accident and was trying to take me somewhere to get help. She's quite an actress, Patsy is, and wearing Mom's clothes, carrying me...well, it worked. It shouldn't have, but it did. It worked for ten long years."

"Nobody ever checked on Patsy's car? The one that was left on the side of the road? Saw the damage? I mean, there must have been damage to the front end, where she rammed your car."

Emily turned her head, looked at Josh. "Deductive reasoning," she said, smiling ruefully. "Now I know where Toby got it from. Yes, they checked on that car, but it was stolen—Patsy had stolen it—and it had been wiped clean of prints. The conclusion was that some teenagers had stolen the car, gone joy riding and then panicked, run, after hitting our car.''

''Panicked. But took the time to wipe off any fingerprints. You know, Emily—Miss Colton—if anyone ever wants to go handing out blame or feeling guilty about how easily Patsy Portman carried this whole thing off, there'd be a long, long line of candidates for the honor.''

Emily nodded. ''I know. But you have to remember something else. This was Joe Colton's wife. Senator Joe Colton's wife. All he cared about was Meredith, and me. We were all right, and an investigation, even an arrest, would have plastered the whole thing all over the newspapers. Mom—Patsy—asked him to let it go, told him the only thing that mattered was that she and I were all right. He listened to her, and the police listened to him. Case closed. Oh, and you can stop calling me Miss Colton. I think we've gone beyond that, don't you?''

''Don't you, *Josh,*'' he answered, throwing back the sleeping bag and reaching for his boots. ''All right, *Emily.* How about you get the camp stove lit and boil us some water for coffee, while I take care of the horses. As you might have noticed if you lifted your nose a fraction, it's time to muck out the cave.''

Emily smiled evilly, somehow feeling much better. Good enough to tease. ''Gee, I thought that was you,'' she said, then pulled the covers over her head until he'd grumbled, then walked away. Only then she did dare to emerge from under the sleeping bag cover, find her own boots and warm coat, and then go search out the travel packets of instant coffee she'd luckily packed in her backpack.

Fifteen minutes later, she and Josh were sitting cross-legged on the sleeping bag, sipping steaming coffee. "I hope you don't need cream, because I don't have any. I always take mine black."

"This is fine," Josh said, taking another sip from one of the chipped ceramic mugs Emily kept stored in the plastic container. "I guess it's time for that inventory now. I've got beef jerky, some packs of instant oatmeal—although we might want to check the expiration date—and a bag of M&M's."

"A bag of M&M's? That's all you have?"

He shrugged rather sheepishly, and Emily had to look away, because he looked so damn appealing, even with—or maybe because of—his morning beard.

"Hey, I didn't plan on being out here. The way I figured it, I'd see you, talk to you, and be back in my bunk at Rollins Ranch before nightfall."

Emily tipped her head to one side, looked at him closely. "Yes, about that. How did you know I was coming up here? Did you *follow* me?" She sat back. "You did. You *followed* me. I sort of thought you might have, and maybe you even said something about it. Yes, I'm sure you did. But I was too upset and cold last night to give it much thought. You *followed* me, Josh Atkins. How could you *do* that?"

"Because we need to talk," he answered, returning her stare. "Because I need to know how Toby died, *why* Toby died. I want to know why he thought you were worth dying for, and I by God sure want to know how you could leave him there on the floor, dying, and just walk away.''

Emily shook her head. ''No. I can't talk about that. I will not talk about that.''

''Funny,'' Josh said, getting to his feet, looking down at her. ''I don't remember giving you a choice.'' He walked to the mouth of the cave, flung the contents of his mug into the rain, then pulled his slicker off the makeshift clothesline. Shrugging his arms into the slicker, he bent low, ducking under the rope, and went out into the storm.

To get away from her? To calm down, cool down in the slashing rain, before he touched her...shook her until she told him what he wanted to know?

Emily wasn't sure.

Rebecca looked up from the grant application she was trying to decipher, and smiled as she saw Martha Wilkes walk into her office. ''Back so soon?'' she asked teasingly. ''And why aren't I surprised?''

Martha dipped her head slightly, smiled. ''I take it you were expecting me.''

''Oh, yeah. I was expecting you. Tatania, on the other hand, was just plain *hoping* you'd be back. You two really hit it off, you know. Not that she's started chattering like a magpie, but she is interacting more with the other children since your visit yesterday. She even told Billy Rogers to shut up when he began singing during grace at dinner last night. Quite the little mother, our Tatania. I think, given half a chance, she'd soon be the leader in her age group here at Hopechest. I—we *all* can't thank you enough."

"I just talked to her," Martha said, ever modest about her own skills. "That's all she really needed. Someone to talk to her, someone to listen."

"We all talked to her, Martha," Rebecca reminded her. "We all listened, not that she said anything. No, you did something special, and if we could bottle it, all the kids here would be the better for it."

"Thank you," Martha said, giving in, not wishing to hear more, as she hadn't come here this morning for praise. "Rebecca? I was wondering..."

Rebecca folded her hands on the desktop and leaned forward slightly. "Are you going to ask if we could use another volunteer around here? Because if you are, the job's yours. The pay is lousy—nonexistent—but the fringe benefits are great. I already spoke to Blake—that's Blake Fallon, he runs the place—and he said I should put you in a half Nelson and *drag* you back here until you agreed to help us."

Martha frowned. "Fallon? Would that be any relation to Emmett Fallon? The man who tried to kill Joe?"

Rebecca nodded. "Yes, Blake's his son. Emmett was never a great dad, and Blake actually ended up as one of Mom and Dad's foster children, like me. Blake considers running Hopechest part of his payback to Mom and Dad for, as he tells it, saving his life. Ironically, it was Blake's devotion to my dad that pretty much sent Emmett over the edge, so that he tried to kill him. Blake's still dealing with that, poor guy. I think he's afraid he could end up like his dad, but that will never happen. Blake's one of the good guys."

"Circles," Martha said, shaking her head. "It's amazing how everything goes in circles. Circles within circles." She smiled slightly, looking at Rebecca. "And one of those circles expanded to bring me here, to California, to the Hacienda de Alegria, to Hopechest Ranch—to Tatania. Do you believe in fate, Rebecca?"

"Around here, it's kind of hard not to," Rebecca told her seriously. "What are you saying, Martha?"

Martha took in a deep breath, let it out slowly. "Well, for today, I guess I'm asking if I can visit with Tatania again, maybe take her into town, buy her some ice cream. Talk."

Rebecca bent her head, hiding her expression, then looked up at Martha again, her large, blue-gray eyes sparkling. "I think that would be wonderful, Martha. I think that would be really, really wonderful." She stood up, walked around the desk. "How about I take you over to Blake's office, where Holly Lamb can give you the papers you need to fill out in order to become an official volunteer?"

Martha stood, smoothed down her skirt. "Yes, I'd like that. Let's start making things official. I already took the liberty of seeing about having my credentials transferred to California. But you probably knew that already, didn't you, Rebecca? You already figured out that this may have begun as a trip, a chance to help Meredith—but that it's turning into a lot more."

"Yes, I rather sensed that," Rebecca said, leaning forward to give Martha a quick kiss on the cheek. "You'd be surprised at how easy it is to become a part of Hopechest, to become a part of the Colton family. So welcome home, Martha. Welcome home to you, and to Tatania."

"This might not work out, you know," Martha said quickly. "I know you said Tatania has no other family, but that doesn't mean I'd be approved to—"

"Are you looking for somewhere to live?" Rebecca interrupted as they walked down the hallway toward Holly Lamb's small office.

"I went on the Internet last night, as a matter of fact, and checked out a few properties for sale in Prosperino," Martha answered, feeling her cheeks growing hot. "I wouldn't have any trouble selling my house in Mississippi, and I know of at least two psychologists who've offered to either have me join them here as a partner, or sell them my practice back home. I've made good investments over the years, and can pretty much live off the interest, plus the money I'd get for my house, the practice. And, of course, I could run a small practice out of my new house—I'm looking at properties that include an attached office."

Martha shook her head, smiled at her own daring. "Am I crazy? Am I rushing things? I'm not usually so...so impromptu...but this just, well, this just feels *right* to me, Rebecca. I lay awake all night, going over things in my mind, and this just seems right."

"Someday I'll tell you how I came to be at Hopechest, how I came to be a Colton—and how I met the person who made me whole, the way you've just found Tatania. It always seems right, Martha,'' Rebecca said, ''when we finally find our home.''

Nine

Emily liked camping out in her cave. She liked being alone, having time to think. When you've been raised in a big, loving but loud family—even as much as you loved them—you needed a place that was your own.

Meredith and Joe had understood that, bless them, and Emily had been given permission to be herself, which is the best thing you can be given—the right to be your own person.

But now her "alone place" had been invaded by Josh Atkins. The cave wasn't hers anymore, because he was there. Her morning wash was hurried, she'd felt horribly conspicuous and almost naked just because she had to brush her teeth while he was there. Her trip outside, made in her slicker and damned uncomfortable in the first place, was an embarrassment to her.

She couldn't do this. She couldn't stay here with him, in this cave, until the storm passed.

And she couldn't leave until the storm passed.

She was stuck, she was here, and neither of them were going anywhere.

"That's quite a look you've got on your face, Emily," Josh said as he reentered the cave, slipping out of his slicker. "Almost as if you've been contemplating saddling Molly and heading out of here. But no, I'm wrong. Only an idiot would consider trying to get back to the ranch right now, considering that it's more than a three-hour ride in fair weather."

Emily glared at him, wishing he didn't look so good, so manly, so competent. Or so smug.

"How nice that you don't think I'm an idiot," she told him, her teeth clenched. "It's about the *only* rotten thing you've not thought about me."

Josh hung his slicker over the rope once more and approached the cold campfire. "There's not a dry stick of wood out there, although I am going to take your axe and cut some of the drier underbranches, then drag them in here and hope they dry out enough to make at least a small fire tonight. It'll be smoky, but it's all we've got."

Emily nodded her agreement. "I'll help. There are a couple more caves, higher up on the hill, and maybe there's some dry brush or something that's blown into them. But you'll have to check them out, because there are bats in those caves and I won't go inside."

"Bats, huh? I was wondering why there aren't any bats in this cave, to tell you the truth."

"It's because it's just a small cave, Dad said." Emily looked around her once safe haven, a space that was about the size of a two-car garage, and only about fifteen feet high. "There's a cave up higher that has two entrances, one on either side of the hill. The bats like it better there."

There was a full minute of uncomfortable silence before Josh spoke. "Okay, so we've decided that we're not going anywhere. We are going to try to gather some wood. And we know you don't like bats. I don't like bats, either. Now what? See any good movies lately?"

Emily directed a long, dispassionate stare at this infuriating man, who just smiled back at her. "I thought I'd read my book," she said tightly. "I came up here to be alone, not to entertain guests."

"Especially unwanted guests," Josh replied, his smile growing wider. "But you have to admit, Emily, I do come in handy. I'm taking care of the horses, and I've noticed that you've already ripped into my stash of M&M's."

"You drank my coffee," Emily shot back, then sighed. "Oh, this is ridiculous! I'm not going to talk to you about Toby, so you can just get that idea out of your head. You don't like me, it's clear you don't like me, and anything I'd say would just give you another reason to glare at me like I just crawled out from beneath some slimy rock."

"So you did leave him there to die."

"No!" Emily stood up quickly, headed for her poncho, pulled it on over her head. "But I am *why* he died. Do you think I don't know that? I'm going to look for firewood," she ended, and bent low, slipping under the rope, knowing she'd feel safer out in the storm than she did looking into Josh's eyes.

Austin McGrath pushed the last manila folder into his briefcase and looked across the coffee table at Meredith and Joe Colton. "There's a lot of information here, just as you said, Joe, but I can already think of a few avenues that weren't pursued by any of Patsy's investigators. I'm not proud to say this about fellow P.I.s, but it would appear that the ones Patsy hired were more interested in getting her money and stringing out the investigation than they were in locating Jewel."

Meredith leaned forward on the couch, her hands clenched tightly as she rested her arms on her knees. "Really? Patsy would hate to hear that, she always took so much pride in being smarter than anyone else. But you think you can do it? It was such a long time ago, Austin."

"Over thirty years," he agreed, making a slight face. "However, that might be the one thing in our favor. Adoption law has changed, and many adoptees have begun looking for their biological parents. They've set up organizations, sites on the Internet—and many formerly closed adoptions are now pretty close to public record."

"So Patsy's daughter, grown now, actually might

be looking for her?" Joe put in, also leaning forward. "I hadn't thought about that. She's certainly old enough to be in charge of her own life, make her own decisions about something like this. And she could be out there, looking. Searching the same way Patsy has been searching."

Meredith sighed. "Her father murdered, her mother the murderer. Her lying, cheating father selling her at birth to hide the illegitimate child from his wife and family. Maybe she shouldn't be looking, Austin. Maybe she's better off not knowing. Maybe we're doing more harm here than good."

Joe and Austin exchanged glances, and Austin said, snapping his briefcase shut, "Tell you what, Meredith. I'll look at this from both directions—our hunt of Jewel, and her possible hunt for her biological parents. If I find her, and if her name appears nowhere on any list of adoptees looking for information about their biological parents, then we'll stop right there, possibly reconsider our approach. But if she's already looking for Patsy? If she has indicated in any way that she wants to find her biological mother? Well, then we should probably go ahead. What's that old saying? Better the devil you know?"

"Patsy being the devil Jewel would finally know, the answer, *any* answer, being better than a lifetime of questions," Meredith said, reaching into her pocket for a small white linen handkerchief, then pressing it to her eyes. "Joe?" she asked, turning to look at her husband. "What do you think?"

He reached over, squeezed her hand. "I think we

should let Austin get to work,'' he said, then rose, extending his hand to the private investigator who was also his foster daughter's husband. ''One thing's certain. At least this will all stay in the family. The last thing we need is more press. Austin, thank you.''

''You got it, Joe,'' Austin said, then went over to bend down, kiss Meredith's cheek. ''I'll report back as soon as I learn anything. Just please remember that I'm following an awfully cold trail, so this might take a while.''

Meredith reached up, stroked Austin's cheek. ''I promise not to pester, Austin,'' she said, blinking back tears. ''But we only have a month. Patsy only gave us a month.''

''I'll see your three M&M's, and raise you two. Blue ones. They count as quarters, right?''

Josh picked through his own stash of candies, pushing three red and two blues into the pile on the sleeping bag. ''Quarters, right. That must be some hand you have there,'' he said, inspecting his own cards, three twos and two kings.

They'd found the deck of cards in the plastic container, and Josh had challenged Emily to a few hands of poker, never believing she'd take him up on it. M&M's were their chips, and Emily was beating him, badly. If she'd agreed to strip poker, he'd be down to his shorts by now.

''Call,'' he said, then leaned back, waited for Emily to lay down her cards.

''Full house, queens over tens,'' she said, and he

threw his own cards facedown on the sleeping bag, indicating that he'd lost.

"Let me see," she said, reaching for his cards.

"Hey!" he countered, quickly scooping them up again. "I thought you promised me that you know the rules. You win the pot, not a peek. I'd rather my strategies remained my own, thank you very much."

"Strategy? You have a strategy? What is it—hoping like hell? I'll bet you were bluffing."

Josh looked at Emily, her eyes bright, her smile wide, that glorious hair of hers tumbling down in a warm, living flame. "I never bluff," he said, trying to sound dark and menacing.

"Oh, yeah, right," Emily said with a sniff, gathering up the cards and beginning to deftly shuffle them against her bent knee. "And you never back down, either. Except maybe when you almost walk in on a hibernating mama bear and her cubs. Then you don't back down—you run like hell. Except it wasn't a bear, was it? It was just a shadow."

Josh sucked in his cheeks. "Could have been a bear," he offered weakly, knowing that he'd only pretended to be scared, just so that Emily would react, have a good laugh at his expense, maybe relax her guard a little.

"Could have been a lot of things," Emily agreed, unable to hide her satisfaction. "Luckily, it was a huge rock and a bunch of dry scrub that blew into the cave and lodged against it. The fire is nice, by the way."

"Anything to please the lady," Josh said, picking

up the cards she'd dealt him. He looked at his hand—pure garbage. "You wouldn't be dealing from the bottom of the deck, would you?" he asked as he anted-up—two brown M&M's. "Or maybe these cards are marked?"

Emily sat up straight, sort of wiggled around where she sat, her eyelids narrowed as she deliberately wiped the side of her hand beneath her nose. "Them's fightin' words, cowboy," she told him.

"Oh, yeah? And what are you going to do about it?" he countered, turning his cards around to show her the mess of nothing she'd dealt him. "We haven't even drawn cards yet. Let me see your hand. Now."

"You get the pot, not a peek," she said, repeating his own words to him as she went to pick up the deck, slide her own hand into the pile.

He caught her wrist with one hand and reached for her cards with the other. She wasn't letting go, and she slapped at his hands to make him release her. Within moments, they were rolling around on the sleeping bag, M&M's scattering everywhere, Emily giggling as she fought to keep control of her cards.

Josh got her onto her back, then straddled her, her efforts to free herself beating against him with all the impact of butterfly wings. Within moments he had her cards, then sat back on his haunches, on her, to look at them.

"Four jacks and an ace," he said, shaking his head. "Now tell me these cards aren't marked."

"Well, I did think that was being a little greedy. I was going to take two cards, giving back the ace and one of the jacks,'' Emily said, trying to be sincere, although her giggle sort of ruined her sincerity act. ''Honest.''

''Uh-huh, sure you were,'' Josh said, turning one of the cards over, inspecting the back of it. ''Marked. And not even well. I guess I wasn't paying attention. Damn! Where did you get these?''

Emily lifted her arms to push her curls away from either side of her face. ''Rand, my brother, gave them to me when he was cleaning out his room before he left home. They're ancient, from some bunch of magic trick stuff he'd had stuck in the back of his closet. I just keep them up here if I want to play Solitaire. I forgot they were marked, honest. But...then I remembered.'' She bit her bottom lip, trying not to smile. ''I like M&M's, okay?''

Josh flipped the cards to one side, then took hold of Emily's wrists, pressed them back against the sleeping bag as he bent low over her face. ''You...are...a menace,'' he said, trying to keep his own humor in check. ''What if I had said we could play strip poker?''

Emily lowered her eyelids for a moment, and then he was dazzled once more by the sight of her huge blue, mischievous eyes looking up at him. ''Wow,'' she said. ''Strip poker, huh? Wouldn't that have been something?''

Josh looked at her, feeling the mood change, shift, slide into something not at all teasing. He lowered himself until his face was within inches of hers. She was so soft, beneath him. Her chest rose and fell, and he could imagine how she'd feel through the soft, worn flannel. Her mouth was so inviting.

Another inch. All he had to do was move another inch lower. Close the gap. Taste her.

Emily looked up at him, not flinching, not withdrawing, not trying to free her arms from his grip. She pressed her lips together, the tip of her tongue appearing for a moment as she moistened those lips. "Um...I think...I think you should get off me now," she said, her voice low, nearly a whisper.

"Yeah," Josh said, at last reclaiming at least a small part of his common sense. "I think so, too." He let go of her wrists, reluctantly, then lifted himself off her. "I'll go hunt up something for the horses while you decide what we're having for dinner, okay?"

"Okay," Emily said, quickly jackknifing herself to a sitting position, turning her back to him. "That sounds like a plan."

"Only one I've got," Josh said, heading for his slicker. He should leave it in the cave. He could use a cold shower.

"Rain's stopped," Martha said, standing at the French doors, looking out into the garden as the sky rapidly turned dark. "No stars, though, and no moon. Just what looks to be a bunch of gray clouds hanging low over the ocean."

"Another storm," Meredith said, bending over a box of clothing Joe had brought to her from the basement storage area. "Although this one might actually go south, Joe told me. I hope so. Emily has yet to phone us, and her phone is turned off, so we can't reach her. She'd phone if she had any trouble, I'm sure of that. Joe said reception could be interrupted up in the hills, because of the storm, and— Oh, Martha, I know Emily has a good head on her shoulders, but I still don't like the thought of her stuck out there, unable to get home."

"Yes," Martha said, turning away from the window. "What if she develops appendicitis? What if she runs out of food? What if...what if? Our minds can do terrible things to us, can't they?"

"Well, mine hadn't thought of appendicitis—until now. Thanks so much, Martha," Meredith said with a rueful smile, pulling out a green crewneck sweater with red reindeer running across the chest. "Ah, Joe found the right box. Come here, Martha, and look at this. I made it myself. Every child wore this for at least one Christmas."

Martha took the sweater, the better to admire it. "Meredith, one of these reindeer only has three legs."

Meredith smiled, her face aglow with memories—memories too long hidden from her. "I *did* say I made it myself. It was one of my first efforts, and I actually improved with practice. But Joe says this one is special, just because of the three-legged reindeer, and the kids seemed to agree with him. Michael named him. Hopscotch. Isn't that a silly name? But Michael loved that sweater. He..." Her voice trailed off and she bit her lip, turned her head away from her friend.

Martha put an arm around Meredith's shoulder. ''Sometimes the memories hurt, don't they? I'm sorry.''

Meredith nodded her head, closed her eyes tight. ''He was such a sweet boy. We still miss him, all of us, although Drake was hit hardest of all. His twin, you understand, plus he was there when Michael was run over. So young. Michael was only eleven when he died. So many dreams yet to live. Oh, Martha, you're right. This hurts. Remembering hurts.''

''Should I ask someone to put the box back in the basement?'' Martha asked, folding up the sweater, tracing a hand over Hopscotch, her own tender heart touched.

''No, not yet,'' Meredith said, sitting down on the couch and pulling the box toward her. ''I gave a lot of the children's clothing away, to Hopechest, but I always hung on to some things, some special things. It would seem like I'm going to have too many grandchildren to be able to distribute these old clothes fairly. Besides, each child has already taken his or her own special favorites, a tradition I began before I...before I left.''

She bent low over the box, carefully lifting layer after layer of clothing until she found what she was looking for. ''Here we go, Martha,'' she said, pulling out handmade striped mittens, a matching scarf and beret. The stripes were bright: red, yellow, blue, green.

''You did say the coat you bought Tatania today was red, didn't you? Poor child, shivering in her sweater and just a thin rain poncho, all her clothes lost in the fire that took her mother. I love little girls in cheery, bright red coats. That's what made me think of this set I crocheted so many years ago. I think these will match perfectly.''

Martha accepted the items, her eyes stinging with tears. ''They're beautiful, Meredith. Are you sure—''

''Positive,'' she answered, closing the box again, leaving the reindeer sweater on the couch beside her. ''And Hopscotch, too. Of course, the sweater is only a loan, but none of my grandchildren are big enough yet to wear it, so I'd really like Tatania to have the honor this Christmas.''

Now Martha's tears escaped, and she wiped at them without embarrassment. ''Meredith, I knew. From the moment I first met you, I knew. You're special. You've always been special. And I'm honored to call you my friend.''

''Rain's stopped,'' Josh said, standing at the mouth of the cave. ''If no more storms roll in, we'll probably be able to get out of here tomorrow morning as soon as it's light.''

Emily looked down at her fork, filled with canned ravioli. They'd had ravioli for dinner last night, lunch today, and again for dinner. How she rued the loss of her food bag, and Inez's fried chicken. She'd pay serious money for roast beef, mashed potatoes and gravy. For that alone, she should be happy that the rain had stopped. Even happier that they'd be able to leave here tomorrow.

Her to the Hacienda de Alegria, Josh to the Rollins Ranch, or the rodeo circuit, or wherever he'd head next.

They'd both be free of each other, of this enforced cohabitation that had been anything but easy.

Free to go on their way...with nothing said, nothing resolved...and with him still believing she'd left his brother...her still knowing that she'd been the cause of Toby's violent death.

"That's nice," she said, then lifted the fork to her mouth, the ravioli tasting like sawdust.

Could she do this? Should she do this? Just wait for the rain to stop, and then go home, let him ride away?

He was so like Toby, and yet so different. Where Toby had inspired her friendship, Josh affected her in a much more elemental way.

She'd see his face in her dreams for years to come. She'd hear his voice, recognize his walk, come alert at the special mixture of smells—of horse, of leather, of his shaving cream—that had this unwanted ability to rouse her, make her want, make her need.

It would never work. Not between the two of them. Even if he was all Toby had been, yet so much more. Even if there had been no Toby, and they'd just met, connected, admitted to the electricity that leapt between them with just a look.

They came from two different worlds, she and Josh. Emily knew herself to be a plant that needed deep roots, even if she did like to feel independent.

Josh had no roots, none at all. He went where the wind blew him, where the circuit took him.

Emily couldn't live like that.

What was she thinking? Of course she could never live like that! He hadn't asked her, had he? So why was she even thinking about such a thing? Why was she suddenly so disappointed that the rain had stopped?

"Josh," she said at last, as he returned to the meager fire and picked up his own plate. "I think we need to talk."

Ten

Josh put down his plate, not exactly hungry anyway. "Talk?" he repeated, looking at Emily. Her beautiful face looked white and pinched in the campfire, her burnished curls making a soft halo about her head, turning her look fragile. Vulnerable. "Not if you don't want to, Emily," he heard himself say, unable to believe he actually was about to let the woman off the hook.

What was wrong with him?

Big blue eyes, that was what was wrong with him. That air—more than an air—of innocence. That was what was wrong with him. He'd gone soft, just as his brother, Toby, had gone soft, almost eager to cut this girl some slack, give her every benefit of the doubt, believe her excuses, maybe even her lies.

"Well, no, I don't want to," Emily said, putting down her own plate, laying it to one side as she sat forward, her clasped hands on her knees. "This isn't a matter of *wanting* to, it's a question of whether or not I can live with myself if I don't talk to you."

"About Toby," Josh said, staring at the tips of his boots as he stretched his long legs out in front of him. "Okay. I'll start, because I did want to tell you about him. Tell you about the Toby I know...knew."

"That would be nice," Emily said, her voice small, coming to him seemingly from very far away. "He told me you'd pretty much raised him. Is that true?"

Josh wanted to pace, but he stayed where he was, memories bubbling to the surface of his brain, fleeting snapshots of a younger, smiling Toby flashing before his eyes.

"Yeah, that's true enough, I suppose. Mom died when I was ten years old—Toby was only about six. We had our dad, but drink also had our dad." He lifted his head, looked over at Emily. "He was a good man at heart, but Mom's death, well, it took most of that heart out of him. He'd drink, lose his job, promise to do better. We lost our house, then moved from town to town, from cheaper apartment to cheaper apartment, running out on our rent because Dad had drunk his paycheck. But he was sorry. He was always so, so very sorry. So were we."

"You loved him," Emily said, nodding her head.

Josh rubbed at his forehead. "Loved him? I suppose so. But we'd lost our mother, just like he'd lost his wife. And then we lost our father, too, to the bottle."

"I don't want to interrupt, Josh, but I think I sort of know what happened, not from experience, as I was too young to remember my own circumstances except for what I was told, but because I've seen this sort of thing. We have this place near my home, Hopechest Ranch, where a lot of us in the family volunteer time. A place for troubled children, abandoned children. I've never ceased to be amazed at the maturity of those children who'd lived with an alcoholic parent. They become little parents themselves, taking care of the other children in the family, acting as parent to their own mom or dad. They lose their childhood, and it's sad to see."

Josh felt his jaw tightening. "Toby didn't lose his childhood. I made sure of that."

Emily's sympathetic look set his teeth even more on edge. "Yes, I'll bet you did. Parent to the parent, parent to the sibling. Making the meals, cleaning the house, hunting down the parent at local bars, trying to bring that parent home before the whole paycheck was gone. All that responsibility, and no time for your own childhood."

"I did what I did, and I'd do it again," Josh told her, willing himself to be calm. This wasn't about him, it was about Toby. "And we made it, damn it. Dad died, but not until after Toby had graduated from the local community college and had been accepted at the police academy." He felt a smile tease at the corners of his mouth, surprising him. "He wanted to help people, Toby said. To him, being a policeman meant helping people. He actually believed he could make a difference.''

''Toby did make a difference, Josh,'' Emily said, poking a long, thin stick into the small fire. ''He saved my life.''

Josh looked at her, really, really looked at her. ''Tell me about it,'' he said at last. ''I need to hear what happened. Not the police report version. What *really* happened.''

Emily continued to poke at the fire, her head bowed. ''Yes. It's time, isn't it? I'd like to start at the beginning, if that's all right with you.''

Josh listened to the sound of the howling wind outside the cave. ''Start anywhere you want, Emily. I don't think we're going anywhere for a while. Just as long as you tell me about Toby.''

Emily nodded her head, laid down the stick, carefully, as if it were made of crystal. ''It all really starts months earlier, with my mother's twin sister, and with her plan to kill me.''

Josh remained silent as Emily told him about Patsy Portman. She'd already told him about the planned ''accident,'' of how the switch had been made so many years ago. Now she told him of those next nearly ten years, of how it had been to live in the same house with a woman who looked like her mother, yet, to Emily, couldn't be her mother.

She didn't whine, tell her story as if asking for his pity, but only accentuated the fact that she'd always had questions, reservations about this woman who acted so differently than the loving mother she'd known.

"I had dreams, nightmares really, and they got worse over the years, never better. I began to remember more, question more. One day I spoke with one of our longtime kitchen employees, Nora Hickman, asking her if she saw what I saw." She paused, looked up at Josh. "Three days later, Nora was dead, the victim of a hit-and-run."

"Patsy?"

Emily shook her head. "Only indirectly. She wasn't driving the car, although she did pay for Nora to have some sort of fatal accident that couldn't be traced to her. She left the method itself to Silas Pike."

Josh's hands drew up into fists. "The man who murdered Toby."

"Yes. But nobody had yet identified the driver, or realized why Nora was killed. I certainly hadn't, although I wondered why Nora had died. If I'd believed the woman in our house wasn't really Meredith—if I'd truly *believed* that—I probably would have remembered more of the details of my conversation with Nora and put two and two together. But all I had were my doubts, my fears. Besides, how could I tell my father that I thought his wife wasn't his wife—that maybe his wife was a murderer? Dad wouldn't have believed me. Nobody would believe me. Why should they? Lord knows nobody believed me all those years, all those nearly ten years."

"Because you didn't believe it yourself," Josh said. "It's difficult to believe the worst of your parent, believe it deep in your heart, even when the evidence is right there in front of you.''

Emily's shoulders, that had been nearly hunched as she spoke, visibly relaxed, lowered. ''You understand,'' she said, smiling at him, tears in her eyes. ''I didn't think anyone would understand.''

Josh's smile was rueful. ''Hey, my dad was a fall-down drunk, but I'd challenge anyone who ever looked down on him, said anything bad about him to my face. So you keep on keeping on, part of you knowing the worst, another part of you refusing to believe that same truth. You didn't *know* that Patsy was impersonating your mother. You just knew that your mother didn't seem...right. So if Nora died, and your mother had something to do with it...?''

''I couldn't face that, not at the time,'' Emily ended for him. ''But then Silas Pike was in my room, in the dark, and I could see the outline of the knife he held in his hand. I had been out with some friends and I came into an empty house and was just heading to bed. I saw him from my doorway.''

''God,'' Josh said quietly, shaking his head. ''That's when you ran?''

''I had no other choice. Mom—Patsy—was already hinting to everyone that I was unbalanced. And now I was seeing outlines of murderers skulking around in my bedroom at midnight? I had to run. I had to figure out how to approach Dad, the family—make them believe what I believed. I had to go somewhere alone, to think, to sort everything out.''

''And you landed in Keyhole,'' Josh said, sighing.

''What's that line from *Casablanca?* 'Of all the gin joints in all the world, why'd she have to walk into mine?' Something like that. But you walked into that small café in Keyhole, and into Toby's life. Our lives.''

''Lying,'' she added, when he didn't say the words. ''I came into Toby's life, lying, telling him I'd lost my fiancé in a car wreck, and had come to Wyoming to forget, to try to rebuild my life.'' She ran a hand through her hair, pushing it back from her face as she looked at Josh. ''If I hadn't lied...if I'd told him the truth? If I'd told him that I was afraid, that a killer might be on my tail...?''

Josh did stand up now and begin to pace. He couldn't sit still any longer. ''You had your reasons for keeping silent. I can see that now.'' He stopped pacing, turned to look down at her. ''That night. Tell me about that night.''

''More guilt. Another mistake.'' Emily shrugged, twisting her hands in her lap. ''But first I have to back up a few months. Pike had found me in Keyhole, back in the spring. I came home from the café and he was there...in my house, waiting. I called Toby—'' She remembered the day vividly, would never forget it. ''I got away before he could hurt me and I ran...again. I went north to Montana, and I was there when Rand, my brother, summoned me to Mississippi. He'd found out—doesn't matter how—that my mother was living there, a victim of amnesia.

''That should have been the end of it, but it wasn't. Mom...well, Mom wasn't ready yet to go back to

California, back to her own life. I should have stayed with Rand until Mom was ready to go home, or with my cousin Liza—anyone at all—but I didn't. I went back to Montana, to my life—such as it was. But I—I couldn't stop thinking of Toby. Finally, I felt I owed it to him to go back to Keyhole, to explain myself to him, to say a proper goodbye."

"Because you knew he loved you."

Emily bit her bottom lip, nodded her head. "Yes, because I knew he loved me. I had to tell him that I loved him, too, but that I wasn't *in* love with him," she agreed quietly. Then she looked up at Josh, her eyes pleading with him to understand. "I thought I was safe! I never would have gone back if I didn't think it was safe to do so—never! I wouldn't have put Toby in danger."

"I believe you."

"Wh-what?" Emily blinked back tears as she looked up at Josh, that film of tears softening his features, making him look more like his younger brother. "You believe me?"

"I'm not a total jerk, Emily. I believe you."

"But—but I was so *arrogant!* I never disguised myself, never believed anyone could have followed me, and yet Silas Pike mentioned my hair when he broke into my motel cottage that night. He said...he said people remembered my long hair. I should have cut it, dyed it—something." She shook her head, so that her hair fell forward over her face, hiding her features. "Mistakes. I made so many mistakes, and those mistakes cost your brother his life. Oh, God, Toby, I'm *so* sorry!''

Josh crossed in front of the fire and went down on his haunches in front of Emily, so that they were face-to-face when she finally lifted her head once more. He reached out with both hands, smoothing her hair away from her tear-wet cheeks. ''He knows, Emily,'' he said quietly. ''He knows.''

Emily's sob caught in her throat and she drooped forward, laying her cheek on Josh's shoulder, holding on to him as she cried. Bitter tears, yet cleansing tears, tears Josh wished he could shed himself, because then maybe he'd feel better, less guilty himself.

''That night, Emily,'' he urged her when her sobs had subsided into the occasional sniffle. ''What happened? The police report I read was only preliminary, written before they were able to interview you.''

Emily sat back, leaving him feeling suddenly abandoned as she slid her arms away from his shoulders, settled them in her lap once more. ''I'd taken a cottage at a motel on the outskirts of Keyhole. Toby... We'd made plans to see each other the next day, but he came that night. I couldn't tell him everything that night, it...just seemed too soon. Besides, he was on duty, so there really wasn't time. We visited...and then he left.''

Josh frowned. ''So how did Pike manage to get into your cottage?''

''My stupidity again. I opened the door to him, thinking he was Toby, coming back. Who else could it be, but Toby? I didn't think. I just didn't *think*.''

She picked up the long hem of her flannel shirt, wiped at her streaming tears like a child scrubbing her face. "He burst through the door as I opened it," she said, closing her eyes, making a face. "God, he was so *ugly,* so frightening. He seemed to fill the whole room. And then there was this gun...and all I could see was the gun. It looked like a cannon, a cannon pointing straight at me. He wanted me to turn around, so that he could shoot me in the back, but I wouldn't do that. I refused. And then...and then I sort of dived behind the couch, because I couldn't just stand there and let him shoot me. And then the door opened, and I heard Toby call my name. There were gunshots, two of them. I didn't know what happened, I couldn't see anything. I just cowered there, until I heard a moan. Toby's moan."

"And Pike?"

"He was gone. The door was wide open, and he was gone. Only Toby was there, lying on the floor, this...this..." Her hands fluttered, resettled in her lap. "This *blood* everywhere. I knelt down beside him and he smiled up at me. 'I forgot my hat,' he said. 'I forgot my hat...'"

Emily pressed a hand to her mouth, her eyes seeing another scene, not the inside of the cave, not Josh, sitting so close in front of her. "He'd somehow hit the Alert button on his uniform, so officers had to be on their way—but I knew they wouldn't arrive for at least fifteen minutes, not all the way from town to the motel."

Josh nodded his head. "The panic button. Cops use

it to summon help if they're in trouble. It's part alarm, part locater. But Toby didn't think you could wait for other officers? Did he think Pike was still close by, waiting to take another shot at you?"

"I think so. Toby must have thought so. He reached for my hand, asked me if I'd been hurt. He was dying, and he asked if *I* was hurt. Then he told me to run, to get away, to leave him. I—I couldn't. How could I leave him? I wanted to stay, get him some help, but I think we both knew help couldn't arrive in time, at least not for him. And then...he was gone."

She looked at Josh helplessly. "He was holding my hand, and then he was gone."

Josh lay awake, holding Emily close to him, his heart breaking each time she whimpered in her sleep, still obviously reliving Toby's death in her nightmare.

A hat.

Toby had died because he'd forgotten his hat.

Emily was alive because Toby had forgotten his hat.

How did a person justify such a thing? Calling it Fate sounded like too much, terming it coincidence seemed like too little.

Josh felt something sticking him in the back, and reached under him, pulling out one of the cards they'd played with earlier. He held it up, looked at it, unable to see the face of the card in the darkness, and a thought hit him.

Josh's dad had called it the luck of the draw, as if

life was one big card game. Sometimes you drew well, sometimes you got the Joker. Josh's mother had drawn the Joker, and was dead within months of her diagnosis. His dad had kept trying for the Ace, and Lady Luck had kept dealing him Jokers, too.

According to his father, it just all boiled down to the luck of the draw. Either you had it, or you didn't.

Toby hadn't had it that night. But, then, neither did Emily, and she hadn't been drawing good cards for a long while, a lot of years. Maybe it was just time for her luck to turn good, just as it had been time for Toby's luck to run out.

Don't ask why, say why not. Don't try to rationalize, place blame. All luck isn't good, all the cards we're dealt aren't Aces. All the platitudes sounded so rational, in the dark of the night, here in this cave, Emily lying beside him, her breathing finally soft, and regular.

Josh sat up, held the card closer to the dying fire. What would it be? He hadn't been drawing many Aces himself. Was it time his luck changed?

Squinting, he turned the card toward the light of the fire, then looked at the card for a long, long time.

The Ace of Hearts.

"Damn," he whispered quietly, turning the card over and over in his fingers. He looked at Emily, snuggled under the sleeping bag, her hair not tied back in a ponytail, but spreading against the seat of the saddle—warm, and inviting, and begging for him to touch it, slide his fingers through it, push that length away from her nape so that he could press his lips against the side of her throat.

Toby had loved this woman. Josh desired her. Toby had seen her as gentle, needing his protection. Josh saw her as strong, if troubled. Toby believed he could make Emily love him, be content to settle in Keyhole, raise kids and go to church on Sunday. Josh didn't believe anything, about anything, about anyone.

Toby should have lived. Maybe then he could have convinced Emily that his love was true, that there was a happy ending for the two of them. Then Josh could keep up his rambling, rootless ways, and visit Toby and Emily on holidays, at which time he'd have to crawl into a bottle just as his dad had, to block the sight of Emily and his brother, together, from his mind.

Because he wanted this woman. He wanted her for himself. He ached for her in ways both physical and emotional, and he wanted her for all time. But he knew he couldn't have her, not with Toby alive, not with Toby dead. It just wasn't in the cards for them.

Josh rubbed hard at his closed eyes with thumb and forefinger, then stabbed his hand into his hair. Was he out of his mind?

He tossed the card into the flames, lay down again, and turned his back on the sleeping Emily.

Eleven

Emily stirred in her sleep and opened one eye.

She was on her side. Her *left* side. She never slept on her left side, never.

Worse, she was snuggled up to Josh's back, chest to toes, folded against him, her knees tucked behind his, one arm cupping his waistline.

In sleep she had done what she refused to even think about while awake. She'd somehow gravitated toward Josh Atkins, sought out his warmth, his strength, the very solidness of him. And, once she'd found it, she'd hung on for dear life…and slept soundly for the first time in months, perhaps years.

She closed her eye, rubbed her cheek against the flannel of his shirt, amazed at the feel of taut muscle beneath that soft material. She remembered his body as she'd seen it that first night, when he'd stripped off his shirt before she could avert her eyes, pretend disinterest.

Whipcord lean, not an ounce of fat. Muscles that rippled rather than bulged. Those scars on both his belly and chest. A deep tan that told her he spent long hours working, shirtless, in the sun. A man of iron, from his physical body to his strong mind.

But his eyes were like Toby's, in much more than their color. There was a softness to Josh Atkins, a humanity—even if he tried his best to pretend it didn't exist. He had all of Toby's caring ways—for who had raised Toby, taught Toby, if it hadn't been his big brother? But where Toby had been young, still somewhat unformed, Josh's unprotected life had served to carve the grown man to mimic the strength of granite, the hardness of diamonds.

He was the Grand Canyon, rock that stood strong, even while shaped and carved by storms, by the sheer passage of time. The rivers, the weather, had eroded a lot of his softness, leaving this hard exterior, one that could stand up to threats from without, although he could still be deeply moved, hurt, by the threats from within.

No, his softness, his humanness hadn't been eroded. It had gone inside, hidden in the caves of self-preservation. But it was all still there. It shone in his eyes as he'd spoken about his brother, it had manifested itself as he'd allowed her to cry on his shoulder last night, as he had held her close, comforted her.

His brother was dead, wrongly, tragically, and he had comforted *her*.

Molly whinnied softly, blowing, shifting her feet, and Josh's mount shook its head, its harness jingling. Morning. It would soon be morning. Through the night no more storms had rolled in, and the sun would soon rise.

It would be time to break camp, to head home. This strange, unreal interlude would be over, gone. Lost. Josh's softness, Josh's heart, would go back into hiding, and he'd ride away, go back to his lonely, solitary existence. She'd never see him again.

Toby had so loved his big brother. He'd spoken of Josh often, and he'd confessed that he wished his brother would settle down, leave the rodeo circuit, put down some roots. "He needs the love of a good woman," Toby had told her, half smiling. "We all need the love of a good woman."

Love? Was that possible? Was Josh Atkins the sort of man who could recognize love, would accept it if it was offered? He had to be in his mid-thirties, and had been forced to grow up at an age when other boys were playing Little League and trading baseball cards. And, except for his love for his brother, his heart had been locked away, forced to hide in order to protect him from more hurt, more disappointment.

He'd become a loner, mature beyond his years, hardened by circumstance. Emily had read case histories of children like Josh, even children like Toby. The oldest—the "protector/parent." The younger—the "sheltered innocent."

Toby had grown up wanting to help others, to make a contribution, to make a difference.

Josh had grown up, handled all his responsibilities, and then gone in search of the childhood he'd never been allowed to live. What was a thirty-something-year-old man who had no home, who followed the rodeo circuit, who picked up and dropped odd jobs because it was time to move on, before roots dared to form? Was he a man who kept his troubles packed in his bedroll, and took them with him, to the next town, the next ride, the next woman?

Was this a man a levelheaded, home-loving woman should ever love?

Emily's arm tightened as she kept it wrapped around Josh's waist. No. No, this definitely was not the sort of man she needed, should ever want.

And yet she didn't want to let him go.

Not now.

Not yet.

Molly whinnied again, and Josh stirred, slowly coming awake. He raised his right arm slightly, then held it in midair for a moment, as if giving her the opportunity to roll away from him, before slowly lowering it, his hand seeking and finding hers at his waist, squeezing her fingers. It felt so right, so natural. So much more than she'd expected, so much less than she wanted, suddenly needed.

Emily's blood ran hot, then cold, then hot once more as Josh lifted their joined hands to his mouth, pressed his lips against her fingertips. She felt her bottom lip begin to tremble, closed her eyes tightly to hold back sudden tears.

Josh released her hand as he shifted his long body, removing his heat, and turned over onto his right side, so that they lay facing each other. His eyes were clear, completely awake, and his mouth was so close it would take only a small movement for her to put lips to lips. His arm went around her, as hers had been around him, and he pulled her closer, so that their bodies touched again, this time belly-to-belly.

"Say no now, Emily. For God's sake, say no now."

He barely held her, yet she felt unable to move, to retreat. It was too late for retreat. She could only go forward. An inch, two, and their mouths met, their mouths melded, their bodies melded in the heat of the hottest summer day, right there, right then, on one of the coldest, dampest days in November.

Emily snaked an arm out from beneath the sleeping bag and slipped it around Josh's neck as he moved once more, his mouth never leaving hers, to put her fully on her back. Covering her with his body, his long legs entwining with hers.

She lay against a pair of rubberized ground sheets laid over the rocky floor of a cave, and yet she felt as if she were reclining on the finest goosedown, floating on a cloud, borne up by gossamer wings.

Her body was weightless, yet filled with sensation. The warmth that burned inside her, the chill that somehow accompanied it. The weight of Josh's body against hers, the wild, hungry sensations that accompanied each touch of his hand, each movement of his body.

Their kiss deepened, his mouth, his tongue becoming the center of her universe. She forgot to breathe, didn't need to breathe. She only needed to feel. Feel warm, feel loved...feel alive.

So long. She'd been asleep for so long, lost in her misery, her fears, her regrets.

This man knew. This man understood.

This man could help her, free her, absolve her, cleanse her.

She needed him, needed him so much.

And he needed her, Emily was sure of that. He needed someone to hold, someone to ease his own tortures, understand his grief, and maybe his own guilt.

Two hearts, two souls, came together in the most elemental of ways. Filling, slaking, comforting. Reminding them that life was for the living, life was to be lived, and dreams could only come true if you reached for them, reached for them now.

There was pain, but she didn't care, barely noticed. She'd had so much pain, inside her mind, inside her heart and soul, that this small, fleeting discomfort meant less than nothing. Because now she was whole. With Josh inside her, part of her, she was somehow whole.

His gentleness brought tears to her eyes, his rising passion delighted her, his strong arms held her safe as she soared, flew, scraped the stars so that they exploded around her, within her.

Josh's abrupt withdrawal and shuddering release at first confused her, but she quickly understood, held him even tighter against her, stroked his back, kissed his cheek, his neck, as his head lay heavily against her. His body was fluid now, his muscles smooth, almost slack, and she gloried in the softness of his skin, this new power she had discovered within herself.

She had given, and she had taken. He had taken and given in return. They had a bond now, they shared more than their pain, their grief.

Emily turned her head toward the mouth of the cave and saw the sun, filtered through the towering pine trees, making a bright, dusty path for the dawn of a new day…a new life.

Dawn came early at the Hacienda de Alegria, Martha Wilkes had discovered when she first came to stay with Joe and Meredith. She liked that. Dawn in Mississippi was slower; everything was slower in Mississippi. More leisurely, perhaps, but Martha realized now that perhaps she hadn't been built for leisurely awakenings.

It had taken her nearly fifty years, as a matter of fact, to realize she was awake at all, alive at all.

Now she woke with the dawn, eager to be up, dressed and off to Hopechest Ranch. She'd always liked her profession, believed she did good work, sometimes very good work. But never had she felt as fulfilled as she had these past days, walking with Tatania's hand in hers, Tatania feeling safe enough to talk, to giggle, even to skip in her new shoes.

How strange it had been, that first meeting of woman and child. Somehow Tatania had known, as Martha had known, that they were meant to find each other, feed each other, love and protect each other. The bond was almost instant, and immediately strong. The joy was incredible.

Martha stepped out of the shower, donned underwear and pulled on a thick white terry-cloth robe, then walked to the window that looked out, toward the distant mountains.

What a beautiful world!

Was she rushing things? Certainly she was. If she were her own patient, she'd prudently advise stepping back, moving more slowly, definitely not pinning all her happiness on one small child, the possibility that she could become mother to this one small child, find a home for the two of them, build a life, form a family.

But women did give birth, didn't they? One day a girl, a woman, and the next a mother. Holding a brand-new life in her arms, feeling emotions she'd only read about come flooding in with such a sweet intensity that it brought tears to her eyes, humbled her.

"I've given birth," Martha told the rising sun. "All my life, all my training, all my experience, has been the gestation, and now I have the chance to understand, *really* understand, what I've read, what I've seen and never experienced."

Martha padded over to her closet and pulled out a long wrap skirt fashioned of brown, yellow and white material patterned with giraffes, lions, tigers, animals that freely roamed the Serengeti. She teamed it with a soft yellow Angora pullover sweater, layered two lengthy strands of brown wooden beads around her neck, topped it all off with a longish, loose cape-like cotton jacket of chocolate brown.

Tatania would like the giraffes.

She unwrapped the length of Velcroed terry cloth from her head and checked her reflection in the mirror, assuring herself that her hair was fit to see the day. It was, and after the application of some face powder and lipstick, so was she.

Breakfast, an informal session with Meredith, a call to the Realtor about a house with home office she'd seen last night on the Internet, and then the short drive to the Hopechest Ranch. A full morning, and she looked forward to every minute of it, with a love of life that amazed, astonished her.

Martha knew Inez would be up and about, banging pans, preparing biscuits, but was surprised to see Meredith when she entered the kitchen, sitting at the table, sipping tea.

"Sun's up," Meredith said, smiling at Martha over the top of her cup. "I'm hoping Emily will ride in soon."

Behind her, at the stove, Inez turned to look at Martha and rolled her eyes. "Been up since before the dawn, clucking around here like a hen with one chick."

Martha smiled, took up what had become "her" chair, and thanked Inez, who put a cup of steaming coffee in front of her. "I don't blame you one little bit, Meredith. In fact, I wouldn't say you were wrong if you hadn't slept all night, just waiting for the dawn."

Meredith tipped her head to one side, looked at Martha. "Really? My goodness, who are you? Where's that woman who taught me that worrying and fretting change nothing and only deplete our stores of energy?"

Ducking her head slightly, Martha said, "She's in Mississippi, Meredith, sleepwalking through her days, hiding from her own emotions, thinking life is easier, safer, that way. And she can stay there, thank you very much. I'm—" She raised her head, grinned. "Well, I'm actually looking forward to worrying about Tatania, walking the floor, peeking out the window, waiting for her to come home from her very first date with some downy-cheeked boy I have frightened half to death with my questions concerning how he drives, how fast he drives, and does he know how badly I'd hurt him if Tatania isn't home by eleven o'clock."

"Eleven?" Meredith shook her head. "I didn't let my girls stay out past ten when they first dated. Or my boys. They hated that, but I told them, *I'm* the one worrying, so the sex of the child doesn't mean anything. But goodness, Martha, Tatania is only seven years old. Aren't you rushing things?"

"No, just dreaming about things I thought I'd

never experience. And I certainly don't want to rush things. I want to enjoy every moment, not miss a moment."

Meredith's lovely brown eyes clouded, and Martha immediately realized her mistake. She put out her hand across the table, touched Meredith's arm. "I'm sorry, my friend."

"It's all right," Meredith told her, her smile wan, but there. "Everyone's been filling me in on what I've missed. Although I believe I'm seeing highly edited photographs and videos, so that Patsy doesn't appear anywhere. It's just such a roller-coaster ride of emotions, Martha. Video of Sophie's Meggie being born, learning that old friends have died, seeing weddings of my dearest children only through videos."

Then she smiled. "But I had a wonderful experience last night, after you'd gone to bed. I don't know how he got the idea, or where he and Maya found the time, but Drake unearthed the old film of Joe's and my wedding and had it transferred to videotape." Meredith actually blushed. "Joe and I watched it last night in our room."

Standing behind Meredith, Inez beamed, even as her eyes went bright with tears. "Maya asked me to find that old film when she and Drake first got the idea. She let me see it before Drake gave it to Mr. Colton. You were a beautiful bride, and still are."

"Thank you, Inez," Meredith said, her fingers nervously playing with her teaspoon. "It was so long ago. So much has happened since then. Even seeing the film was like watching two other people, two very different people, which I suppose we were.'' She sighed, deeply. ''We were so young, Martha, so full of big dreams, huge hopes. I wonder, how would we approach those same vows now? Would we mouth them again so lightly, with such confidence, knowing what we know now? I'd like to think so. I'd really like to think so.''

Martha and Inez exchanged looks, and Martha made a mental note to herself, and a silent promise to Meredith. Somehow, some way, she'd prove to Meredith that she and her Joe were still those two beautiful young people, still with so much of a bright future ahead of them.

Neither of them spoke, had spoken for the past hour.

One last breakfast of watery oatmeal, one more trip outside for the both of them. A gathering of firewood, to be stacked in a corner of the cave for the next time. Mucking out the latest ''gifts'' from the horses. Packing up, loading up, getting ready to move out.

To leave.

To go their separate ways.

What had happened between them was obviously not to be spoken about, by either of them. There was no embarrassment, no shame, but there was also no communication. They'd said volumes with their hands, their bodies, but the words remained unspoken, perhaps never to be spoken.

It was a mutual silence, a shared isolation, a separation between what had happened and what would happen next.

Emily took one last look around the cave, wondering if she'd ever come here again, if she could bear to ever come up here again. What had been her blessed solitude had now been shared, and Josh was as much a part of this cave now as she had ever been. A trace of him would always be here. She'd see him across the flames of the campfire, hear his soft breathing in the night. If that was all she'd ever have, then she would not come up here again. She couldn't.

Josh saddled Molly, secured the cinch and led the mare and his own mount out of the cave, into the sunlight. "I'll ride first, and you follow, until we're down out of the hills. Just in case there's trees down, or too much mud."

Emily nodded her agreement, and placed her foot in Josh's cupped hands as he helped her up into the saddle. She followed him as his mount surefootedly picked its way down the hillside, ducking her head as tree branches still dripping with rain brushed against her.

It was dark beneath the tall evergreens, but soon—too soon—it was all sunlight, the whole world seeming to stretch out in front of her, bathed in light, fresh from the rain, a beauty that stretched farther than she could see, all the way to the ocean.

Josh's light touch on the reins drew his mount to a stop, and then he turned the horse so that he was facing Emily. "I'm not going to say I'm sorry, because I'm not," he told her, his voice deep, slightly strained. "If you tell me to go to hell, be sure I'm halfway there. But if you're agreeable, I could come by the ranch tonight in my truck. We could talk. Maybe go somewhere for something to eat."

The newly formed ice around Emily's heart cracked, fell away. She'd been so ready for him to say goodbye, for him to move on, go to the next place, the next town, the next, the next, the next. "Dinner...um...dinner would be nice."

She couldn't see his eyes below the brim of his Stetson, but the slashes in his cheeks, the white of his teeth as he smiled, nearly turned her into a puddle of longing she'd only just begun to know existed. "Yeah, dinner would be good. Are you going to tell your parents about me? About the cave?"

She thought about his questions for a moment, then shook her head. "I don't think so. I'll just tell them I met you in town when I bought my new sleeping bag. Okay?"

He seemed to stiffen in the saddle, and she added hastily, "Josh, it isn't like that. I'm not ashamed, or whatever you're thinking. It's just...it's just that this is *mine*. What happened in that cave happened to me, to us. Where it goes from here, if it goes anywhere, is up to us. You don't know large families, Josh, but I do. Believe me, there's precious little that stays private, and I don't think I'm up to playing Twenty Questions with each and every Colton in the civilized world."

Now a real smile twitched at the corners of Josh's mouth. "Toby could ask enough questions for a family of twelve,'' he said, then lifted a hand, tipped his hat. ''Take it slow with Molly, until she gets her legs back under her after being in the cave. See you to-night.''

And then he was gone, riding off toward the Rol-lins Ranch, and Emily was alone once more. Alone, but not lonely.

Twelve

Josh's first instinct was to run. Pack up, quit his job and head out, get away. His reaction to that strong instinct was to curse under his breath, calling himself ten kinds of coward, twenty kinds of fool.

He shouldn't have done it, shouldn't have touched her. Hell, he shouldn't have stayed in that cave. Not for one night, definitely not for two.

Yes, she'd needed help. Her mare had run off, she was stranded, and hypothermia was only one of the problems that faced her. But she'd made a fire, hadn't she? She'd had a blanket, some canned food, a camp stove. She certainly hadn't fit the usual damsel in distress description, badly in need of a brave knight on his white steed to come charging to the rescue. He could have—should have—delivered the mare to the cave, then headed back down the hill, back to the Rollins Ranch.

He was a cowboy, damn it. He'd been out in worse weather than a Northern California rainstorm. He'd been in snow drifts up to his horse's shoulders, in cold so deep his eyelids nearly froze shut, rain so fierce and mud so treacherous that he'd actually seen cows drown in mud.

So he could have made it back to Rollins Ranch that first night, lightning and falling trees be damned.

Of course, what would have been the point of following Emily Colton, of tracking the woman for days, in town and then in the hills, if he only meant to say hello, go to hell, and then leave?

How he'd hated her, had tried so hard to hate her, blame her for Toby's death. It felt so right to blame her, because blaming himself was like ripping his own heart straight out of his chest.

"He was holding my hand, and then he was gone..."

The police report had been wrong, or just incomplete. She'd stayed. She hadn't run; she'd stayed. Even when Toby told her to leave, to save herself, she hadn't left him there to die alone. She'd stayed with him, comforted him. She'd known help was on the way, help that would definitely be too late for Toby, and might be too late for her.

She did the only thing she could.

Which didn't absolve *him.* He hadn't done the only thing he could. Sure, he'd been making some damn good prize money these past years, and bringing down big bucks from endorsements, storing a lot of it away for the day he'd buy his own spread, bring Toby to work that spread with him. But he'd kept hunting down that next ride, that next gold buckle, long after it had been time for him to stop, to turn the rodeo circuit over to younger men still with something to prove.

If he had only quit, bought that spread. And if wishes were horses, then beggars would ride.

Josh checked his own two mounts Rollins let him keep in the stables, then disconnected the horse trailer from his freshly washed dark-green pickup and headed for the Hacienda de Alegria.

He'd showered and dressed in his best jeans, a black shirt and black leather vest, then pulled on his beige suede, sheepskin-lined jacket and donned his freshly brushed black Stetson, the one he kept for special occasions. He was as dressed up as Josh Atkins ever got, and he was pretty sure he'd look as out of place in the living room of the Hacienda de Alegria as Senator Joe Colton and his wife would look in a honky-tonk rodeo bar, tossing back shots of rock 'n rye.

So that was his first shock, and a rather pleasant one, when Meredith Colton herself opened the door to his knock. She was better-looking than the grainy newspaper photos depicted her, slighter in build, yet with a strong chin and wise, intelligent brown eyes. And she was dressed casually, in a red-and-white checked flannel shirt and a pair of jeans that had seen a good amount of wear.

"Hello, you must be Josh," she said, smiling up at him in welcome. "Please, come in. My husband very much wants to meet you."

And that was Josh's second shock, coming to him while he was still trying to recover from the first one. After all, he'd seen the Hacienda de Alegria from the hills, seen its beauty, the massive scope of it. There was money here, lots of it. He hadn't expected a room designed more for comfort than show. He certainly hadn't expected down-home people, a friendly greeting. Not when this footloose rodeo rider had come to call on the cherished daughter of that house.

"Josh Atkins," Senator Joe Colton said, rising from his chair and advancing toward Josh, his right hand held out in greeting. "I saw you ride in Tulsa a few years back. You took the bronc ride, and the overall that night, as I remember it. You sure can sit a horse, son. Welcome to our home."

Josh allowed his hand to be enveloped in Senator Colton's large paw, saying, "Thank you, sir. I didn't know you followed the rodeo."

"I follow a lot of things," Joe said, motioning toward a drinks table, wordlessly asking if Josh wanted anything to drink. Josh just shook his head.

"He does, you know," Meredith told him, patting the sofa cushion next to her, so that he knew he was expected to sit down, probably begin being grilled by one worried mama. "Joe is interested in just about everything. It certainly leaves few gaps in dinner table conversations. So, Emily said she met you in town. You're Toby Atkins's brother?"

Well, that was quick and to the point! "Yes, ma'am, I am."

"Your brother saved our daughter's life," Joe said, taking up his own seat across the coffee table. "This entire family is very deeply in your debt, son. That said, if there's ever anything we can do for you, anything at all, you just have to name it. You're family now, son, whether you like it or not, actually. Isn't that right, Meredith?"

"It's exactly right, darling," Meredith said, reaching over, patting Josh's hand.

"Thank you, Senator…ma'am," Josh said quietly.

"Joe," Joe said, "and I'll beat my wife to the punch on this one, and tell you to please call her Meredith. We're not much on formality around here. Now, are you sure you don't want that drink?"

Josh smiled, shaking his head. "Some ice water, Sen—Joe, if that's all right?"

"Coming right up," Joe said, heading for the drinks table once more. "Which is more than I can say for Emily, as memory serves. The only way to get her someplace on time is to tell her the movie starts at six, not seven. Then, if you're lucky, she'll be ready by six-thirty."

"Oh, good, and get my baby pictures out now, too, why don't you?" Emily said, walking into the room, her lovely face pulled up in a comical, self-deprecating grimace. "Or maybe the ones where I was wearing braces and had hideous pigtails. That ought to do it."

She continued walking toward the drinks table,

kissed Joe's cheek and took the glass of ice water he'd just poured. "Hi, Josh," she said, approaching him as he stood up, pretty sure he should be standing if Emily wasn't sitting.

She looked great. Beyond great. She wore her hair down, that living waterfall of warm fire that fascinated him. She had on a bright blue sweatery-like thing that was all sort of soft and fuzzy, wearing it over a denim skirt that just about hit the tops of her knees.

It was the first time he'd seen her legs, and all he could remember was how they'd felt that morning, wrapped around him.

Josh ducked his head quickly, a sharp sort of nod, and said, "Hi, Emily. You look very nice."

Oh, that was cool. Real sophisticated. What the hell was the matter with him? He'd bedded this woman, for crying out loud. And it wasn't as if he hadn't dated, and very often bedded, more women than he could reasonably be expected to remember in his thirty-five years. So what was wrong with him? What the hell was wrong with him?

"Thank you. And you're about to sit on your hat," Emily told him laughingly as she sat down in the chair next to Joe's and Josh went to reclaim his seat on the couch.

Josh quickly righted himself before he could crush his Stetson, and then he just stood there, looking at the laughing Emily. Wanting to just eat her up…

"Joe?" Meredith said, rising from the couch. "Wasn't that the dinner bell I just heard ringing?"

Joe frowned, glanced down at his watch, looked confused. "The dinner bell? Now? No, I don't think—"

Meredith came around the coffee table and slipped her arm through the crook of her husband's elbow. "Well, I do," she said, maneuvering him toward the hallway leading to the dining room. "Josh, Emily," she called back over her shoulder, "have a nice dinner, you two."

Josh reached down and retrieved his Stetson as Emily stood up, smoothing her skirt. "Want to get going while the getting's good? There's a whole houseful more of Coltons who could be wandering in here at any moment."

Josh didn't have to be asked twice, and didn't really exhale comfortably until after he'd helped Emily up into the passenger side of his truck cab, then settled himself behind the wheel.

"I have *no* idea what just happened in there," he said, inserting the key in the ignition, then turning to look at Emily. "Do I look sixteen all of a sudden? Is there a humongous zit flashing neon red on the end of my nose? Am I speaking in complete sentences, without a lot of *ums* and *ers* and *golly-gee-whizzes*?"

Emily reached over and patted his arm. "Sort of overwhelming, aren't they? And that was only two of them. I'm used to it, grew up with it, and can't tell you how much happier and, well, warm the house is now that my real mother is back with us. But take Mom and Dad, multiply them by all the rest of the assorted Coltons—real, adopted and assimilated, as

Mom calls it—and you can understand why I like my cave.''

Josh started the truck, headed out of the drive toward the highway. ''They're good people, they really are. I don't think I've been around many other people like them. I was welcomed, with both arms. No questions, no looking down their noses at the rodeo bum—nothing. They...knew about Toby, that he's—that he was my brother.''

Emily nodded in the dark. ''Yes, I told them this afternoon. I explained that you often find work on ranches when the rodeo circuit travels somewhere you don't want to go, and that we met in town, at the sporting goods store. They think it's all a happy coincidence.''

''Thank you, Emily. I don't think I would have gotten such a friendly greeting if they'd known I came here purposely to stalk you.''

''No, I suppose not,'' she said quietly, and Josh turned to look at her.

''What's wrong? Should I have kept my mouth shut about that stalking business? Oh, wait, I get it. I still haven't apologized for the way I was all over you that day down at the stables. That was mean, and low, and I am sorry, Emily. I was sorry the moment I opened my mouth.''

''Thank you. I didn't realize I wanted to hear that until you said it. Remember, Silas Pike stalked me, too. So, yes, thank you. Are you hungry?''

''Truth? For a while there, before I met your parents, I believed I might never be able to eat again.''

"And now?"

He grinned at her. "And now I'm starving. Do you know of any steak houses around here? I'm thinking in terms of a hunk of meat too big for the plate."

"And rare, of course, right? Big and juicy and rare on the inside, well done on the outside. Yum!" Emily snuggled against the bench seat, her fiery hair flowing over the collar of her coat. "I know just the place."

Did the man have any idea of the effect his smile had on women?

Emily did her best not to stare daggers into the back of "Hi, I'm Missy, and I'll be your server tonight," as the curvy blonde wiggled her way across the room to turn their order in to the kitchen. When Emily had asked to hear the specials for the night, Missy had immediately turned to Josh and recited them in a Marilyn Monroe-like breathy voice, as if listing her own body parts and their particular talents: "A pair of plump, juicy chicken *breasts, spread on a bed* of *wild spiced* rice, and accompanied by a basket of *fresh, hot buns.*"

It was to gag, or so Emily decided, but when she realized that Josh was totally oblivious to Missy's culinary seduction, she just grinned up at the waitress, thanked her kindly and ordered the prime rib, rare enough to moo.

She leaned forward, putting her elbows on the table, resting her chin on her cupped hands. "You have no idea what just went on here, do you?" she asked, marveling at Josh's composure as he sipped beer from a frosted mug.

"Huh? Oh, you mean Missy? The waitress? Sure, I knew. How old is she? Twelve? I'm thirty-five, Emily. I don't rob cradles."

Emily sat back in her chair. "I'm twenty."

Josh cocked his head to one side, grinned at her. "Really? Maybe I should have asked to see your drivers license?"

"Very funny—not. And Missy has to be at least twenty-one, or she wouldn't have been able to serve your beer."

This was silly, stupid. Why was she talking about the waitress, for crying out loud? Why was she telling Josh her age, almost daring him to tell her she was too young for him? Why was she picking a fight? Because that was what she was doing, wasn't it? Picking a fight?

"You know, Emily, if Missy had been orphaned, adopted, traumatized by a car accident that seemed to rob her of her mother, lived the next ten years in fear and confusion, thrice damn near been murdered by some hired killer, and had a good man die in her arms, well, maybe then I'd say she was old enough, mature enough. And I could be wrong, but I don't think our bubbly waitress has had anything more traumatic happen to her than losing a fake nail in someone's Caesar salad. You may be twenty, Emily, in years, but I think you've paid your dues. I think you're all grown up."

She blinked back quick tears, made herself busy

rearranging the linen napkin on her lap. ''And how old has life made you, Josh?'' she asked quietly.

''Ninety. Sometimes six, or maybe fifteen. Or did you think I didn't know that?''

She looked up at him then, drawn by the sadness in his voice. ''Are you still hungry?'' she asked, wishing away the table that stood between them.

''Not at all,'' he told her, pulling several twenties from his pocket and laying them on the empty charger plate in front of him. ''Let's get out of here.''

He held her hand tightly as they left the restaurant, a bubble-gum chewing Missy watching, eyes wide, as they swept past her as she carried two salads to their table.

Emily giggled at the sight of the waitress, and was laughing in earnest by the time she and Josh had run across the parking lot to the pickup, his arm around her shoulders as they nearly staggered in their mirth.

She piled into the front seat, breathing hard, and waited for Josh to pull open the driver's side door, collapse against the seat before fishing in his pocket for his keys. She could see his face clearly in the lights hanging over the parking lot. ''Where to?'' he asked her, his piercing blue eyes looking straight into hers, straight through her.

''Don't ask me that,'' she said, suddenly serious. ''Just do it, okay?''

He tossed his Stetson into the rear seat of the large cab of the pickup and turned the key in the ignition, tires squealing as he pulled out of the lot.

Five minutes later, Emily saw the neon sign of a

motel, and the smaller, blinking Vacancy sign beneath it.

Ten minutes later, Josh was putting the key into A16.

A heartbeat later, Emily was lifted high in his arms, being carried over to the bed after he kick-slammed the door behind them.

How much better it was when they didn't talk. When there was no reason for words, nothing misunderstood about what they both wanted, what they both needed.

Emily surrendered to Josh's mouth, but only momentarily, before she became aggressive, deepened the kiss herself, until their tongues sought, and found, and dueled. She pushed him away from her, came up to her knees, so that he followed her, mimicked her actions.

Together, they undressed each other. Together, they ripped at the covers, pushing the bedspread to the floor, tugging down the tightly tucked sheets. Together, mouth to mouth, chest to chest, they fell against the bed.

He traced her skin with his strong, work-roughened hands, his mouth following where his hands had been, and Emily threw back her head, her throat tight, memorizing each sensation, each new high that he brought her to, took her past on the way higher, higher.

No longer a virgin, and damned if she'd just be a passive partner, Emily put her hands on Josh, her fingers spread as her palms made contact with his bare chest. What he did to her, she did to him, and when she felt the muscles over his belly tighten she knew he was feeling what she felt, traveling the same path she traveled.

Her hands went lower as he hovered above her, tantalizingly close, still maddeningly separate from her. She touched him, caressed the smoothness of him, silk over steel, and Josh moaned deep in his throat, pulled her on top of him, brought her close for his kiss.

"I thought this could happen again," he breathed against her ear, "and I'm prepared for it this time. But not if you keep touching me like that, Emily. I'm not that strong, not when you touch me."

Emily pushed herself away from him, so that she straddled his hips in the darkness, that darkness, and her desire, erasing the last of her inhibitions. "You mean like this?"

Josh growled, then took hold of her hips and gently pushed her back onto the bed. "You're a heartless woman, Emily Colton," he told her, reaching for his discarded jeans and the small packet in his front pocket. Moments later, his arms were around her once more, and he half lifted her so that she straddled him yet again in this new and exciting intimacy.

She braced her straightened arms on the bed on either side of his head, lifted herself up slightly, then lowered herself again, felt that still-new yet somehow familiar pressure, felt herself becoming one with Josh, a part of him, as he was a part of her.

Would always be a part of her.

Thirteen

Emily lay curled against him, one leg casually thrown over his, her fingers drawing small, tantalizing circles on his bare chest. Her head fit perfectly into the hollow below his shoulder, and her hair felt warm and silky against his skin.

Heaven in the Byde-A-Wee Motel.

Josh idly rubbed his hand up and down Emily's bare arm, pretty sure he'd just made another major mistake in his error-ridden life.

He had nothing to offer this woman. Nothing. And yet he'd taken, taken with both hands, and wanted nothing more than to take again...to hold her, love her, let her heal him.

"There's a rodeo near Phoenix next week," he said, hardly able to believe his own words. "I'm thinking of leaving my job and heading down there. Rollins knew it was only temporary, so there's no problem there."

He felt Emily stiffen inside the circle of his arm, and her hand went still, her palm laid flat against his chest. "Oh," she said, her voice small, hurt.

"Yeah." Josh shifted himself on the bed, pushing himself upward, so that he half leaned against the headboard, pulling her up beside him. "I haven't ridden the circuit since...well, you know. Time I was back at it. I've got sponsors who pay me some fairly nice bucks for wearing their gear, their logos. I've got contracts. I'm expected to make appearances, at least at the major rodeos."

"I see. And this is a major rodeo?"

"Semimajor," Josh told her. "I've been away too long, long enough for my aching muscles to not only heal, but grow soft. I really should get back in the action."

"Yes, I suppose so," Emily said dully. There was silence in the motel room for long moments, before she added, "When will you leave?"

Josh couldn't seem to do much in the way of forming complex sentences. "Pretty soon, I guess. It's a long drive."

Emily seemed similarly afflicted. "Yes, I suppose so. A long drive."

"I could probably stay a few more days," Josh heard himself say, mentally kicking himself for holding out hope—to him, or to Emily, he wasn't sure.

"That would be nice," she answered quietly.

"Will you be back? Will...um...have you thought about coming back?"

His arm tightened around her and she lifted her head slightly, peered up into his eyes. "You know I shouldn't, Emily. We both know I shouldn't. Hell, I shouldn't be here now. *You* shouldn't be here now."

She pushed away from him, sitting up, and shoved her hair away from her eyes. "Why? Why shouldn't we be here, Josh?"

He sat up straighter, doing his best not to look at Emily as she sat there, her upper body exposed to him without shame, probably without notice. God, she was perfect. Everything he'd ever wanted, ever dreamed of, when he had dared to dream.

"You know why, Emily."

"Our ages? Is that it? I thought you said that wasn't a problem."

Now he did look at her, straight into her eyes. "You know it's not that. I—I just don't have the right." He struggled to find the right words. "We met for all the wrong reasons, and I'm a bastard for what I've done, for kissing you, for—"

Emily interrupted him with one word: "Toby." As if suddenly noticing her own nakedness, she reached down, pulled the sheet up and over her breasts. "That's it, isn't it, Josh? Toby."

He raked both hands through his hair, pressed his head back against the headboard. "Damn it, Emily, yes. Of course it's Toby. He loved you."

"I see," Emily said, drawing the sheet even closer. "And you don't. Yet you—you *had* me, and Toby never did. Tell me, Josh, was taking me to bed the way you decided to punish me, make me feel even more guilty?''

''No!'' Josh sat up, took hold of Emily's upper arms. ''God, no, Emily. I wanted you the moment I first saw you, and I kicked myself all the way back to Rollins Ranch that day, because I knew I wanted you. How could I do that? How could I betray Toby that way? Not once, but twice. And damn me, Emily, I'd do it again. That's the worst of it. I'd do it again.''

''Take me home, Josh,'' Emily said, moving away from him, dragging the sheet with her, as if mortified by her unclothed state, embarrassed to let him see her—or perhaps feeling unclean wherever his eyes could see her. ''Just take me home.''

''Emily, I—'' He reached for her, but she slipped away, began picking up her clothing before he could get untangled from the blanket. ''Emily, for God's sake—''

''Oh, no,'' she said, whirling around to face him, her sweater and skirt clutched in her hands. ''Not for God's sake, Josh. Not for Toby's sake, and most definitely not for mine. You took what you took, Josh, and you knew what you were taking, knew what I was giving. You *knew*.''

Her virginity. She had to mean her virginity.

Josh reached onto the floor for his jeans, pulled them up hastily, then grabbed Emily's arm before she could disappear into the bathroom to get dressed.

''Let go,'' she said through clenched teeth.

"I can't, Emily," he said, pulling her into his arms. "I can't let it end this way."

Her body slumped against his, her head pressed into his shoulder. "But it has to end, right? Because of Toby."

He bent down to kiss the side of her throat, rubbed his hands up and down her back. "Because of Toby. He's dead, Emily, and the first thing I do is to move in on the woman he loved. What kind of brother does that make me? What kind of man?"

Emily pushed at Josh's chest, hard, so that he let her go, stepped back to see the fury in her eyes. "I don't get you, Josh, I just don't get you. First you come here to make me feel guilty about Toby, and now it's like you believe you should turn me into some vestal virgin or something, forever untouched in memory of your brother. I loved Toby, he was a fine, fine man. But if you're building a shrine to him, Josh, don't try to make *me* into one of the statues!"

The bathroom door slammed behind her, and Josh slowly walked over to the bed, sat down on the edge, dropped his head forward into his hands.

She was right. Emily was right. The world hadn't stopped when Toby died. Just his world, and Josh's world.

Emily would love someday, be loved again someday. She'd marry, have children of her own—all of that possible because Toby had given his life to protect her, to make sure she had that "someday."

But not him. That man, the man she made that new life with, couldn't be him.

The bathroom door opened once more, slamming back against the wall, and Emily stormed into the room, her burnished curls wild around her head, her slim body tensed, ready to go on the attack.

"And another thing, Josh Atkins," she said, walking toward him, pointing a finger into his face. "Tell me what would have happened if Silas Pike had never found me and you'd come to visit Toby in Keyhole while I was still there. What if you'd looked at me then, and *wanted* me, as you said you wanted me? Would you have walked away because Toby loved me, knowing I didn't love him? Well? Would you?"

He looked at her for long moments, biting back the word *no* that had so quickly leapt into his mind. *No, I wouldn't have walked away. Not if you wanted me, too. Because you were never right for Toby. You're right for me. Even as I'm so very wrong for you.*

Josh stood up slowly, reached for his jacket. "I'll take you home now, Emily."

Josh left the Rollins Ranch two days later, his horses loaded into their trailer, heading for the main highway. Emily knew this because she'd returned the favor—become a stalker in her own right. She'd ridden Molly both mornings, an Inez-packed lunch tied to her saddle, and spent hours sitting on the hillside looking down at the Rollins stables.

She'd felt foolish, she'd felt stupid. But she'd done it, just to see if he meant what he'd said, if he'd really leave.

Leave without saying goodbye.

At ten o'clock, that second morning, she'd gotten her answer.

By noon, she was back at the Hacienda de Alegria, sitting out on the patio near the fountain, her jacket wrapped tightly around her in the chill air, her fists jammed into the jacket pockets, her chin resting on her chest. She didn't know why she was sitting there, how long she would sit there, or if the answer to either question meant more than a hill of beans.

She'd given herself to a man who couldn't give back. How was that for stupid? World-class stupid.

She stretched her jean-clad legs straight out in front of her, lay her head back against the chair, looked up into the watery November sun.

Funny. The sun still came out, didn't it? The world kept on turning on its axis. The chrysanthemums in the garden still bloomed, red and orange and gold. And yet her world had stopped, turned gray, and her mind...? Her mind had closed down, leaving only her emotions. Her hurt.

"Mind if I join you?"

Emily sat up quickly, startled, and saw Dr. Martha Wilkes standing next to her chair, her smile soft, gentle.

"Um, no," Emily said, getting to her feet. "I don't mind. Why would I mind?"

Martha smiled, pulled up another chair and sat down, motioned for Emily to sit again as well. "Oh, I don't know, Emily. Maybe it's because you've been avoiding me ever since I got here, knowing that Meredith and Joe hoped you'd talk to me."

''Avoiding?'' Emily repeated, feeling her cheeks growing hot. ''Oh, no. I haven't been avoiding— Okay,'' she agreed, nodding her head. ''I've been avoiding you. I'm sorry.''

''And so am I,'' Martha told her, reaching over to pat her hand. ''Our discussions, if you decide to consult me, should begin with you *wanting* to talk, being ready to talk. Therapy can't be forced, Emily, by either side. I would, however, really like to get to know you better, if only because you mean so much to Meredith.''

Emily's chin hit her chest again as she looked at Martha out of the corners of her eyes. ''She's worried about me, isn't she? They're all worried about me. I'm sorry.''

''Sorry that they're worried, sorry that you're giving them reason to worry, or sorry that you're sorry? Because you do sound more than a little angry, you know.''

Emily turned her head, grimaced at Martha. ''Is it too much to ask that they just leave me alone? No, don't answer that one. I'm a Colton, and that's the same as saying my whole life is an open book for every other Colton. Not only do they read it, but they also make notes in the margin, then have a discussion that would put one of Oprah's book reviews to shame.''

''So why do they do that, Emily, do you think? Because they're a nosy bunch—bossy and manipulative—or because they love you?''

''I'm getting the idea you don't ask questions unless you already know the answers, Dr. Wilkes. It's because they love me, of course."

"I don't know all the answers, Emily. For instance, are you angry that they love you?"

Emily shot out of her chair, took a few steps, then turned to glare down at the psychologist. "I'm angry that they never believed me," she said, surprising herself with her own vehemence. "Ten years, Doctor, and they never believed me. They taught me how to ride a horse. They taught me to think for myself. They gave me love, they gave me everything. They did everything but *trust* me to know what I saw that day. None of this had to happen, damn it! Not Patsy, not Mom being so lost. Not Toby dying—"

She shut her mouth quickly, put both hands over her mouth as she stared at Martha, then slowly dropped her hands. "What did I just say?"

Martha patted the arm of the chair, urging Emily to sit down again. "Quite a lot, I'd say, my dear. You said quite a lot. Do you want to talk about this some more?"

Emily sat down, moving slowly, feeling fragile, like an old, old woman with brittle bones. "Yes. Yes, I do. I—I didn't realize I was so angry." She turned to look at Martha. "I love my family, Doctor. I love them all so much."

"But families aren't perfect," Martha said, nodding her head. "They make mistakes, most times out of love, sometimes because of their own denial of events, happenings, beyond their ability to understand them, believe them. You *all* suffered a terrible loss,

Emily. All of you. But let's think about that for a moment, all right? Tell me, why do you think Joe and everyone else didn't believe you?"

"Because I was just a kid," Emily said quietly.

"And later? When you weren't a kid anymore? Why didn't they believe you then? Why couldn't you go to Joe, to one of your brothers or sisters, and tell them about the man you saw in your room? Why did you run away from your family, rather than toward them?"

Emily blinked back tears that stung at her eyes. She knew the answer, had discovered that answer in the cave, talking with Josh. "Because I didn't really believe it myself," she said, then sighed. "I'd begun to think Patsy *was* my mother, but that something had happened to her, happened to her head, the day of the accident. I believed she'd become mean, heartless, even mentally ill, dangerously ill." She looked at Martha. "I believed my own mother wanted me dead. How could I say any of that to my father?"

"So you ran," Martha said, folding her hands in her lap. "You ran, and you hid, and you were finally proved right when Meredith was found in Mississippi. Were you angry with your family then?"

Emily shook her head. "I was happy," she said, smiling wanly. "I was *so* happy." She was silent for a while before adding, "Until I went back to Keyhole and Toby got shot saving my life." She looked at Martha. "Sophie says he was a hero, and if I try to blame myself for his death, I'm stripping Toby of his sacrifice, making him into just another victim. He *was* a hero, wasn't he?"

"Yes, I'd say he was, and is, most definitely a hero. What does his brother say?"

"Josh?" Emily bent her head, played with the strings on the hood of her jacket, winding them around her fingers. "He...Josh says it's all right. He understands. He's proud of his brother."

"As well he should be. Is that all?"

Emily wet her suddenly dry lips. "I don't think I want to talk anymore, Doctor. Is that all right?"

"Is it?" Martha asked in return, and Emily smiled, shook her head. "No? I didn't think so. I've been told that Toby was in love with you, but that you considered him just a good friend. Your good friend, Josh's brother. You and Josh. You share Toby now, don't you?"

"Share him? No, Doctor, I don't think so. Josh can forgive me—has forgiven me—for Toby's death. I've even begun to forgive myself. But Toby loved me, and that means that Josh can't." She looked at Martha as she wiped tears from her cheeks with the cuff of her jacket. "Is that fair? We both loved Toby, but does that mean we have to give up any chance of our own happiness?"

Martha sat back in her chair, looking contemplative. Obviously she hadn't known all the answers. "You and Josh...you've had more than a single dinner together, haven't you?"

Emily gave a short bark of laughter. "Oh, you could say that, Doctor. You could say that we've had a whole lot more than a single dinner together. And now Josh is gone, saying there's no future for us because of Toby. I wish he'd never come here. I wish we'd never met."

"Josh has issues of his own, doesn't he?"

"Issues?" Emily dragged her hands through her hair. "Is that what they call taking a woman to bed and then telling her there's no future for them? Issues? Used to be, we just called men like that lousy no-good bastards."

"Yes, or vulnerable souls with things to work out, pain still to be worked through, and time needed for healing before the future can possibly be thought of in any really coherent way. Does he love you?"

Emily pulled a crumpled tissue from her pocket, blew her nose. "I don't know."

"Do you love him?"

"Love him? How could I love him? He left, didn't he?"

"Yes, he did leave, but for what reason? To protect himself, or to protect you?"

"How does leaving me protect me? I talked to him, and he listened. I thought he understood. In this whole mess, he was the one person I could really talk to. There was this...this *bonding*. From the moment we met." She leaned forward, elbows on her knees, and looked at Martha. "It was like I'd met the other half of me, Doctor. Even as I hated him, I knew I needed him. And he felt it, too, he had to have felt it. So how could he walk away? How could he leave me?"

Martha closed her eyes a moment, collected her

own thoughts. ''Emily, you sometimes leave this rather lively household and go off on your own, don't you? To think. You need that time, cherish that time, and that very aloneness feeds you, strengthens you, helps you. Perhaps Josh also needs some alone time right now, some time to think, be by himself, work things through inside his head and heart. You'd understand that, wouldn't you?''

''Yes,'' Emily said slowly, nodding her head. ''I'd understand that. Josh has been traveling the rodeo circuit for a lot of years. You've got a lot of alone time doing something like that, and except for Toby, I don't think he's the kind that needs to be surrounded by others all the time.''

''So if he's upset and confused, he wouldn't immediately call two dozen of his closest friends, to talk about it?''

Emily's eyes softened, and she actually smiled. ''No. I wouldn't either. It's something else we have in common, I suppose.''

''Something besides Toby, you mean.''

''Yeah,'' Emily whispered, turning her head, looking out toward the horizon.

''You know, Emily, I'm a therapist. I'm not a fortune teller. So I can't tell you if Josh will ever come back, because I don't know that. But you do. Deep in your heart and mind, you know. I'd like us to talk some more, Emily, about your family, about Patsy, about Silas Pike...and about Toby. I think you know you need to talk more about everything that happened. We all need time to heal, Emily. You do, Josh does. Maybe the timing wasn't quite right for Josh to come into your life, but someday it will be. You'd want to be ready for that, wouldn't you?''

''And if he doesn't ever come back?''

''You'll want to be ready for that, too, my dear.''

''Yes,'' Emily said, sighing, but lifting her chin, feeling some of her old fight oozing back through her body. ''Yes, I do, Doctor. I need to find *me* again, before I can be any good to anyone else.''

Fourteen

The days were creeping up on Thanksgiving, and the Hacienda de Alegria had begun to swell with children and grandchildren come to celebrate the holiday.

Emily's cousin Liza had flown in with her baby, her husband staying behind and not due in until the day before the holiday. That gave Liza plenty of time to devote to the care and feeding and not always diplomatic prodding of Emily, who just couldn't seem to feel the same ease in telling personal secrets she and Liza had shared since childhood.

"Liza keeps asking me about Josh, and I keep changing the subject," Emily confided to Dr. Wilkes, who she now called Martha, as they'd spoken every day for the past week and had become friends. "Why am I doing that? I've never had secrets from Liza."

"What secret are you keeping from her now?" Martha asked, picking up her teacup as she and Emily sat together in the living room, just before bedtime, the large house quiet at last.

"That I'm talking to you about him, for one," Emily said around a mouthful of peanut butter cookie. "Umm, these are better than good. Inez has outdone herself. She's always baking all my favorites. I think I've gained five pounds this week."

Martha smiled. "Don't tell anyone I said so, but I think that's the plan," she told her, reaching for a cookie of her own. "Not *my* plan, because I could easily do without another five pounds myself. But I think I'm either going to have to develop a lot more willpower, or you're going to have to gain at least another five pounds so Inez backs off."

Emily grinned. "It's a conspiracy, is it? I thought so. And not that I'm complaining. All my clothes were getting too big for me, and I had to put another notch in my belt. I just had no appetite. Lately, however, I think I could eat anything that isn't nailed down. Why is that?"

"You're happier? More at peace with yourself? I should be walking around here, patting myself on my own back, for my brilliance?"

Now Emily laughed out loud. "No wonder you and Mom get along so well. You're as bad as she is. But seriously, Martha—I *am* feeling better. I'm sleeping more soundly, I've got an appetite, I'm not hiding in my room with the house full of family. Can it really be this easy? Talking to you, listening to myself as I talk to you—it really works?''

''That's what they told me in shrink school,'' Martha joked, then sobered. ''You're a strong spirit, Emily, and you'd already gone a long way toward healing yourself. I just helped put on a few of the missing touches. So, tell me about Josh. Have you found anything else about him on the Internet?''

Emily popped the last of the cookie into her mouth, dusted her fingers together to get rid of any crumbs. ''I already told you he took the overall in Phoenix. He didn't do quite as well two nights ago, in San Antonio, but he did win the calf-roping outright, and piled up a lot of points toward the national title. Which he's won twice, if I didn't tell you that before.''

''You did,'' Martha answered, smiling. ''Twice, as a matter of fact. So where is he now?''

Emily frowned. ''I don't know. The rodeo moved on to Oklahoma, for an indoor show, but he isn't listed for any of the events.'' She shrugged her shoulders. ''So I don't know where he is.''

''Could he be coming here?''

Emily picked up another cookie, turned it back to front as if examining it for an answer. ''I don't know, Doctor and Soothsayer. Could he?''

''Let me check my tea leaves,'' Martha said, lifting the empty cup and peering into it. ''Darn, no tea leaves. I guess I'm going to have to wing this one, huh? Do I think he's coming here? Better question—do I think you're *ready* for him to come here? And the answer to that is, yes, I do. And, before you ask again, if Josh Atkins is half the man you tell me he is, I expect to be meeting him one day soon."

"Not that I need him to be complete," Emily said, her chin tilted up defiantly.

"Absolutely not."

"And not just because we went to bed together."

"Not since the old days of shotgun weddings," Martha agreed, smiling. "Although maybe you shouldn't try asking Joe about that one."

"And not just because I love him," Emily ended, sighing. "Oh, Martha, I do love him. I barely know him, but I love him. Unbelievably, I actually think I love him enough to let him go, which probably makes me certifiable, huh?"

Martha picked up the plate and held it out to Emily, grinning. "Don't think too much, my dear. Here, have another cookie. It'll be one less that I eat."

Josh drove through the night after leaving San Antonio, finally pulling over into a rest area when he felt his eyelids beginning to droop, sleeping a few hours in the cab of his truck, then getting back on the road again.

He'd left his horses and trailer with friends in the rodeo, knowing they'd be taken care of, and headed north with just his truck, his saddle and the jumble of clothes he stored in the cab. He traveled as he always had: alone, unencumbered.

And for the first time in his life, he felt lonely.

Another long drive, another few hours in a roadside

motel, and by late the second day he'd arrived in Keyhole.

Toby's rent had been paid until the end of the year, and Josh still hadn't had the guts to go through his brother's personal effects, sort them, pack them away, so he headed straight for the apartment, planning to do just that.

Do that, and a few other things.

He pulled the key from his pocket and let himself into the apartment, his nose wrinkling as he smelled spoiled fruit, soon locating a bowl of nearly disintegrating apples on the kitchen counter.

Still wearing his Stetson and jacket, Josh opened all the windows, then rummaged through cabinets until he found a supply of plastic garbage bags. He tossed in the apples and what probably was once a banana, all the contents of the refrigerator and the kitchen trash can, then took the bags down to the Dumpster in the parking lot, disposing of it all.

Toby had kept his apartment neat, orderly, so it wasn't as if he'd walked into a mess. He had, however, walked in on a lot of memories Toby had spread through the rooms: photographs on every table, his sports equipment stacked in a corner of the living room, a framed magazine cover that showed Josh after he'd won his first national championship.

Josh stood in the middle of the room. Where did he go with everything? What did he do with it all? How did he get through this without breaking down, losing it?

"First, I eat," he said out loud, and headed to his

truck, driving to the Mi-T-Fine Café where Emily had been employed, where she and Toby had met.

He sat in the last booth, his back to the wall, barely tasting the hamburger and fries he'd ordered, watching as people came and went, living their lives.

Toby's people. These were the men and women and children Toby had sworn to protect and serve. Nice people. Nice town. No one would think violence could ever come here, but it had. It had come, and it had gone, and life was moving on.

Josh's next stop was the local grocery store, where he loaded up on some lunch meat, bread, milk, a dozen eggs and an angel food cake, just because it appealed to him. Then it was back to the apartment, where he unloaded the food and his duffel bag, planning to crash on the couch rather than sleep in his brother's bed.

He sat on that couch as the night grew dark, not bothering to turn on any lights, but just sitting there, his hands on his knees, remembering. Toby with his two front teeth missing. Toby riding his first horse. Toby in a rented tux, taking Mary Sue Potenski to the prom. Toby in his sheriff's uniform, a pistol strapped to his leg, his smile so wide and proud it had made Josh's heart ache.

And the other memories. Toby crying for his mommy, who was never coming back. Toby small and scared and climbing into bed with him when their dad came home, roaring drunk. Toby hungry, and with nothing in the house to eat. Toby bravely smiling, saying it was all right if Santa forgot them this year. Toby holding his hand, walking beside him, depending on him, believing in him.

"Oh, God. Toby. Toby..." Josh said, leaning forward, dropping his head into his hands as, at last, after keeping all his emotions inside, locked up, hidden away, he cried for his brother.

Rebecca came up beside Martha, standing with her as the two women watched the kickball game in progress in the small gymnasium.

"Who's winning?" she asked, nodding her head toward the action.

"Tatania, mostly," Martha said, pride in her voice. "Oh, she hasn't scored, but she's out there. She's playing. She's interacting with the other kids. I consider that a victory all by itself."

"And we take our victories where we can find them, don't we?" Rebecca said, smiling. "Are the two of you going to town again this afternoon?"

"Yes, we are. Tatania has an appointment with the judge, thanks to all the red tape Joe was able to cut for us. She's going to tell him whether or not she wants to come live with me. Forever and ever, as Tatania says. Not that this will all happen overnight, of course, even with Joe's recommendations." She turned to Rebecca. "Although I have bought a house."

"You have? Oh, Martha, that's wonderful!" Rebecca said, hugging her friend. "Where?"

"Just outside Prosperino, in a lovely new development of single homes. It's not quite complete, so

Tatania can pick the color of the carpet for her room, the colors for her bathroom, and there's an attached office, with zoning allowing professional businesses. There are already two doctors in the development, and I understand there are quite a few software designers working out of their homes."

"Are you talking east of the city? Because I think I know the area you mean. Those are huge homes, Martha. Huge and lovely."

Martha grinned. "It is big, I agree, but I have a feeling we'll be able to fill the rooms over the years. Tatania's told me she wants a big family. Besides, there's a community pool, and horseback riding trails, a lovely pocket park, and good schools close by. I think the judge will be impressed," she ended, sighing happily.

"I think the judge will ask you if he can move in, too," Rebecca said. "Seems you and Tatania will have a lot to be thankful for this Thanksgiving."

"I can't begin to articulate how much, Rebecca," Martha said, then clapped and called out encouragement as Tatania gave the ball a good kick and scored a point. "Meredith tells me we'll have about forty for Thanksgiving dinner. Can you believe that?"

"Yes, I can. Small crowd. It seems some of us won't make it back home until Christmas this year," Rebecca told her, grinning. "This is our first big Thanksgiving in a long time, as we didn't really have family gatherings when Mom was gone. Just society parties Patsy enjoyed and we all hated. But that's all over now, and we're back to big, noisy get-togethers and Drake and Rand fighting over drumsticks. I can't wait!"

"Rebecca?"

Both women turned to see Blake Fallon's secretary, Holly Lamb, approaching them, her pretty face looking troubled.

"What is it, Holly?" Rebecca asked, and Martha quickly recognized the concern in her voice.

"It's the kittens, Rebecca," Holly told her, her eyes moist, as if she was fighting back tears. "You know how the children were so excited that Boots was having kittens? They all wanted to name them, see them as soon as they were born?"

"Yes, I know that. Boots should be giving birth any day now. So what's wrong?"

"They're dead, Rebecca. Boots had six kittens this morning, out in the barn, and they're all dead."

"Oh, God. None of the children saw, did they?"

Holly shook her head. "No, we took care of it. But isn't that strange, Rebecca, that all of them would be born dead? And you know we've been finding dead mice in the barn, and sometimes just lying around on the ground, as if they just lay down and died. It doesn't make sense, does it?"

Martha looked to Rebecca, waited for her answer.

"No, Holly, it doesn't make sense. I've been assured there are no poisons in the barn, or anywhere else at Hopechest, for that matter. Have you told Blake?"

"Yes, and he said not to say anything, at least not

to anyone except you and a few others. But he's definitely going to start some sort of investigation."

Martha stepped forward a pace. "What about the children? Are any of the children sick?"

Rebecca shook her head. "No, not really. More than our usual run of colds, runny noses, but we did have a lot of damp, rainy weather this month. Oh, and Billy George has pneumonia. He was admitted to the hospital this morning, and he's going to be fine. Why? Surely you don't see a connection between some dead mice and kittens, and the children?"

"No, I suppose not," Martha said. "Sorry, Rebecca, it's just this new and highly sensitive mother-mode I've seemed to have developed since meeting Tatania. Don't pay me any attention at all—although I'm glad to hear that Blake is taking this seriously enough to start an investigation."

Josh stood in front of the stone marker, looking down at the inscription placed there and paid for by Toby's fellow officers, at their insistence. Toby's name, dates of birth and death were there, and one more thing, the words "A hero fallen in the line of duty. Always to be remembered."

Always to be remembered. That was nice. Josh put down the bouquet of flowers he'd brought, placing them beside others that still looked fresh. Toby was being remembered.

There was a small American flag stuck into the ground beside the gray granite stone, a flag that would probably be replaced once a year, donated by the women's auxiliary of some civic group or another.

Josh raised his head, looked out across the small cemetery. Neat. Orderly. Graves marching in curved rows, trees and benches scattered about, many of the graves marked with fresh flowers.

A peaceful place.

A place Toby Atkins didn't belong, not for at least another fifty years.

"I love you, buddy, and I miss you," Josh said, then turned away, headed back toward his truck, parked on the narrow macadam drive that wound through the cemetery.

Someone was standing beside his truck, a man dressed in the same sort of uniform Toby had worn with such pride. A blue-and-white police car was parked behind the truck, as if the officer had stopped to check up on the strange vehicle in his town's cemetery.

"Afternoon, Officer," Josh called out, donning his black Stetson once more, narrowing his eyelids as he looked at a kid as young and fuzzy-cheeked and earnest as Toby had been. "Can I help you?"

The officer leisurely pushed himself away from the side bumper of the truck, his hand held out to Josh. "You're Toby's brother, right? I think I remember you from the funeral. Good to see you."

"Good to see you," Josh answered automatically. "You worked with Toby?"

"Oh, yeah, we all did. One hell of a sheriff, one hell of a guy. See the flowers?"

Josh involuntarily looked over his shoulder, toward the headstone. "Yes, I saw them. Why?"

"Oh, no reason. Get new ones every week, you know, from that Emma Logan—Emily Colton, I mean. Regular as rain, every week, new flowers. She's got some sort of deal set up with Flossie, down at the flower shop. Isn't that something? He was crazy about her, you know. Just crazy about her."

Josh ducked his head, a muscle working in his left cheek. "Yes, I'd heard that. He was in love with her."

"Love? That so?" The officer reached up a hand, scratched under his hat. "Don't know how's I'd exactly call it love. More a sort of worshippin' from afar, as my wife called it. He had that girl on such a pedestal, none of us think he'd have known how to handle it if she ever even hinted that she wanted... you know, more?"

Josh rubbed at his forehead, kept his eyes averted. "So they didn't...date?"

"Date? Good God, no. Toby drank coffee at the café, took to visiting her at night, checking up on her safety he called it. But that's it. He knew it wasn't going anywhere, but that was all right by him. My wife thought it was really romantic, you know? Women, what do they know, right? Well, I gotta get moving. School lets out soon, and with old man Baxter laid up with a broken leg, I'm in charge of the school crossing on Seventh." He tipped his hat, headed for his truck, calling back to Josh, "Nice seeing you. And don't you worry none, we're still watching over Toby, and always will.''

"Thank you,'' Josh said, then watched as the squad car backed up, pulled out onto the narrow roadway and drove away. "I mean it, you know,'' he said after the officer was gone. "Thank you. Thank you so much.''

It was time to pack up Toby's things. Sort them out, give his clothes to the local charity, donate the furniture, hand the key back to the landlord. It was time to accept what couldn't be changed, and get on with life. Never to forget his brother, never to fully get over the loss, but definitely time to let go of the bad, start reaching for the good. Wasting his own life wouldn't bring back his brother, wouldn't honor the memory of his brother. Even a fool such as himself knew that.

Suddenly, he knew a lot of things.

Toby hadn't loved Emily, he hadn't understood her. If he had, he'd know that she was a woman, all woman, and that the last thing she needed, or wanted, was to be put on a pedestal, worshipped as if she were some fragile angel who couldn't be touched for fear she'd melt away.

Emily needed to be loved, everyone needed to be loved, but she also needed to feel alive, desired, not worshipped. She was flesh and blood, not gossamer.

And she'd been right. If Silas Pike had never come to Keyhole, if Josh had come instead, to visit his brother, he would never have walked away, leaving

Toby to his first puppy love, and Emily to her pedestal.

He would have moved in, taken, shown Emily desire, fed their mutual hunger. And sure, it would have hurt Toby. For a while. There would have been no avoiding that.

But it would have happened. As sure as he knew his own name, he knew Emily was right, and it would have happened. She was his other half, she was the spark that made him come alive, she was feelings and needs and even demands, and he had recognized her the moment he first saw her, because even without knowing it, he'd been looking for her all of his life.

So what the hell was he doing with motel reservations in Tulsa?

Not much. Not with his truck heading toward California.

Fifteen

Meredith snuggled close to Joe, her cheek against his chest, sated and happy in the afterglow of loving. They were like newlyweds again, making love every night, sometimes during the day, when Joe would come find her, take her hand, lead her to the bedroom.

They laughed, even giggled together, couldn't get enough of each other.

And the deep worry lines around Joe's mouth had begun to soften. The nightmares had disappeared, both his and hers. They fell asleep in each other's arms, woke happy to greet each new day.

But this grand new life, this second chance, was not without its worries. Life was never without worries, Meredith knew. Still, shared worries were easier to carry.

And shared joys were that much happier.

"Emily's smiling again," she said as Joe yawned into his hand. Honestly, the man seemed to think he could survive on five hours of sleep a night and considerable "exercise" while in his bed. Not that Meredith was complaining. "Joe? Did you hear me? I said, Emily's smiling again. And eating."

"You didn't say that the first time. The part about eating," Joe told her, ruffling her hair. "See? And you accused me of not listening."

"My apologies," Meredith told him, snuggling closer. "But you do agree with me, don't you? Martha won't say anything, and I don't expect her to breach a confidence, but I think she also believes Emily is coming to grips with what happened, beginning to get on with her life."

"We all knew she would," Joe said. "Emily bounces, she doesn't break."

"And Emily is in love," Meredith told him, just because he sounded so smug. "You knew that, too, didn't you?"

Joe moved to sit up against the headboard, slightly dislodging Meredith from her comfortable position. "In love? With whom? The only person I can even think of is Josh Atkins, and they only went out to dinner that one time before he left town so it couldn't be— Is it him?"

"Liza thinks so, and unlike Martha, she isn't bound by professional privilege. You know, I'd like to be around to plan at least one of my daughters' weddings. Not that I would ever picture Emily wanting a huge wedding.''

''How do you women do it?'' Joe asked, sitting up even straighter. ''One date, and you're planning a wedding. I barely know this boy.''

''It's not you who has to know him, Joe. Or don't you trust Emily to make good decisions?''

''Got me again, didn't you?'' Joe said, sighing, pretending to be insulted. ''So, if you're right, and Emily and Josh *are* going to get together, all I can say is that I'm glad my tux still fits. It's gotten quite a workout lately.''

''I always thought you looked so handsome in formal wear, darling,'' Meredith told him, reaching up to pat his cheek. ''Even if those tight collars always make your face go a little red.''

''A little— Hey! I thought you said I looked handsome.''

''And you do, you do, but you're twice as handsome in a soft shirt and a nice sweater. More cuddly.''

''Cuddling's good,'' Joe said, reaching for her, but Meredith held him away, knowing she had something else to tell him. She'd saved the news all day, holding it close, waiting until Joe was relaxed, ready to listen.

''Austin phoned earlier today,'' she said, which effectively halted Joe's next romantic move. ''He has some news.''

''Already? I didn't think he'd be this quick. Good or bad news?'' Joe asked, pulling back the covers, slipping his arms into his bathrobe. ''No, wait, let me get a drink of water, and I'll be right back.''

Meredith just nodded, knowing he was using the excuse of being thirsty in order to give himself time to shift gears, talk about anything that had even remotely to do with Patsy. If it were up to Joe, Patsy's name would never be mentioned again in this house, in his lifetime.

"Okay," he said a few moments later, reentering the room from the bathroom. "What did Austin have to say?"

Meredith also got out of bed, pulled on her dressing gown and came to sit with Joe at the bottom of the mattress. "He says he thinks he may have found Jewel."

Joe took a sip of water, then held on to the glass with both hands. "Okay. Now the big question, Meredith. Was she already looking for Patsy?"

"Yes," Meredith said, her eyes stinging with tears. "Yes, she was. So now we have to decide, Joe. We have to decide if Jewel should know about Patsy, about Ellis Mayfair. It's a lot to handle, for anyone."

"And it's not really our decision, sweetheart," Joe told her, looking deeply into Meredith's eyes. "Is it?"

"No, I suppose not. And there are Joe, Jr. and Teddy, Jewel's half brothers. How can we deny any of them that sort of knowledge?"

Joe slipped his arm around Meredith's shoulders. "Looks like all our questions are already answered, sweetheart, and any decisions already made. I'll phone Austin in the morning, let him get the ball rolling. Where is she, this Jewel?"

"Ohio. Medford, Ohio. A long, long way from Prosperino. She was adopted—Austin called it a black-market adoption—and her adoptive parents kept the name she was given, Jewel Mayfair, and added their own name, Baylor, to the mix. The bad news is we can't go after the terrible lawyer who forged all the necessary papers that made it seem legal for Jewel to be placed for adoption, because it all happened so long ago. He would have had to know that Ellis was dead, that Patsy was in jail. So he'd have had to have forged any signatures."

"Yes. Ellis must have had the papers all drawn up before the birth, so only the name and sex had to be filled out the day Jewel was born, the same day Ellis delivered her to the lawyer. And the lawyer would have had adoptive parents all set and ready to go, and collected all the money, including Ellis's share. Nice day's work, the bastard."

Meredith nodded, for Joe had said much the same things Austin had said, both men having come to the same conclusions. "But the Baylors probably never knew they were part of anything illegal."

Sighing, Joe drew Meredith closer to him. "Well, that's all water under the bridge, as the saying goes. Jewel has to be in her early thirties now, and Austin says she is searching for her birth mother. So we bring her here, as our guest, and break it to her gently about her parents once we've welcomed her to the family. Because she is family. Can you handle this, babe?"

Meredith slipped her arms around Joe's waist, gave him a squeeze. "I can handle anything, darling, as long as I have you. And I already told Austin you'd probably be phoning him in the morning. It's nice to know that I still know you so well. You've a good heart, Joe Colton. A good heart."

Thanksgiving morning dawned bright and sunny after two straight days of rain, which was a good thing, because the younger members of the Colton family had all begun suffering some fairly major cabin fever and needed to be outside, playing off some of their built-up energy.

Joe, Jr. and Teddy had already escaped to the lawn with Rand's adopted son, Max, five years old and a perpetual motion machine in jeans and a Washington Redskins sweatshirt. Joe had brought along his football, and the three were throwing—and mostly chasing after—the ball, laughing and giggling and pretty much being all-American kids. When Wyatt and Annie Russell's twin sons, Alex and Noah, joined the other boys, and Drake, Wyatt, and Rand got into the action, the game truly was on.

Inside, in the spacious living room, Thad Law's daughter, Brittany, was, at the ripe old age of nearly five, putting herself in charge of Sophie's daughter, Meggie, and Drake and Maya's beautiful little girl Marissa. It was Brittany who doled out rattles and balls, and then took them away again when the mood struck her. Lana Reilly, pregnant with twins, sat on one of the couches, shaking her head at the scene. "And I thought someday I wanted six or more children? I believe I'm going to have to rethink that one and get back to you all later, say when the twins are in kindergarten."

Sophie James reached down to bring her unhappy child up and onto her lap, handing over her daughter's favorite thing in the whole world, her rawhide teething ring. "Oh, don't plan that far ahead, Lana," she told her. "Motherhood, I'm learning, is pretty much a one-day-at-a-time thing, at least when they're this young. Now, if you want to start talking braces and college funds, well, that's when River and I start getting the shivers."

Liza walked into the room and collapsed into one of the overstuffed chairs. "Whew, that's one down, hopefully to sleep for at least an hour. Thank heavens that child of mine still believes in morning naps. You know, ladies," she said, gazing down at the chubby-cheeked children on the carpet, "we really have to get a family photograph. Wide-angle lens, of course, to get us all in."

"Especially me," Lana said, putting both hands on her swollen belly. "Where are Emily and Amber? Don't you think they'd want to baby-sit, so that we can all head for the kitchen and another cup of tea? It would be good practice, especially for Amber."

"Amber? Baby-sit?" Sophie said, smiling at the babies. "I don't think she's planning this far ahead yet. But wait, maybe we have a volunteer," she said as Emily wandered into the room. "Em? Want to baby-sit while the rest of us girls run off to some warm, tropical island?"

"Or the kitchen, which is closer," Lana said. "I'm not quite built for bikinis right now."

Emily laughed, then sat down on the floor beside Brittany, who was stacking blocks for Maya's daughter's edification. "You know, we've got people missing for Thanksgiving dinner, but everyone has promised to be here for Christmas. Can you imagine the madhouse? Mom's loving every minute of it. She and Inez are in the kitchen now, basting two of the biggest turkeys I've ever seen. Amber's setting the table, and I came to hide out in here, sort of blend in with the crowd, hoping nobody finds me and puts me to work."

As if on cue, Meredith walked into the living room, wiping her hands on a dish towel. "Emily? There's a huge bag of vegetables in the refrigerator with your name on it. How about cutting up some carrots and celery?"

"Oh, darn, Meredith, the one thing I'm good at, and you're giving the job away," Martha Wilkes said, entering from the foyer, Tatania holding tightly to her hand. "Tatania? Would you like to stay with the babies while I help out in the kitchen?"

Emily looked at Martha's foster child, soon to be legally adopted child, and her heart melted. What a sweetheart! Dainty, quite petite, with huge light brown eyes framed by the thickest, longest, most curly lashes she'd ever seen. Tatania looked at the people sitting together in a group, then up at Martha. "Can't I stay with you?"

Martha bent down, so that she was face-to-face

with Tatania. "Sure, sweetheart, you can stay with me. But you don't have to. You can do anything you want."

Tatania tipped her head to one side, obviously in deep thought, for she'd been given a choice. Better, she'd been given the right to choose. "Okay, then I'll go back outside and watch the football game. They're funny."

She turned and ran toward the door, Martha calling after her that she shouldn't forget her jacket, and then the doctor looked at the assembled women and shook her head. "I'm learning who you all are, and rather proud of that fact, but I'm not quite sure just who goes with whom. So...which one is Chance?"

"He's mine," Lana said, not quite able to keep the pride out of her voice.

"Oh, really? Well, in that case, maybe you ought to know that he made a wonderful, diving catch just as Tatania and I arrived, then landed face-first in a rather large mud puddle. Then your husband," she said, turning to Sophie, "piled on top of him, and the two started rolling around in the mud. By the time I could pull Tatania away, I believe Joe, Jr. and little Max had joined in."

"Oh, this I've got to see," Sophie said, getting up from her seat, holding Meggie on her hip as she headed toward the front door. "Ladies, shall we all go take a look? And hope that the garden hose is still connected out front, so we can wash them all off?"

Emily stayed where she was as everyone else gathered up babies and went to see what was going on outside, her knees bent beneath her as she gathered blocks and began stacking them.

"Emily?" Martha said, coming over to the couch and sitting down for a moment. "How are you doing today?"

"Fine," Emily said brightly. Too brightly. "That is, I'm okay."

Martha nodded her head. "Lots of couples here today, aren't there?"

"Hanging from the rafters," Emily agreed, knocking down the small tower of blocks. "I've asked Amber to set a place for me at the kiddie table."

"Because you're the only one without a partner?"

"Yeah," Emily said, getting to her feet. "Something like that."

Martha rubbed a hand over her mouth, looked up at Emily, her friend and patient. "Holidays can be a hard time to be alone, Emily. This isn't a setback, it's a rite of passage."

"I know, and I'll be fine," Emily assured her. "But I had this little...fantasy. I thought I could introduce Josh to everyone today. I guess that isn't going to happen."

"It may never happen, Emily. You know that, we've discussed that."

Emily squeezed her hands together in front of her. "Oh, I'm just so *mad* at him! How can he know what we had and then walk away? I mean, fine, great, go somewhere, get your head screwed on straight. That's okay. But then come back. Even if it's only to say 'Sorry, Emily, this isn't going to work out.' He could at least have done *that,* couldn't he? Don't I deserve at least *that?*"

Martha stood up, put an arm around Emily's shoulders and said wryly, "Well, it would appear we've passed beyond the self-pitying and mourning stage, and gone on to anger. Believe it or not, Emily, acceptance comes next."

"Oh, really?" Emily said, pulling away from Martha's gentle touch. "Well, I'm not ready for that yet, let me tell you! I'm mad, Martha. I'm really, really mad at him." Her shoulders slumped. "It's easier to be mad at him."

Martha gave her a kiss on the cheek. "I'll go cut up those vegetables, Emily, and you go wash your face, maybe take a walk, all right?"

Emily touched her cheeks, realized they were wet. "Oh, Josh Atkins," she said, shaking her head, "you don't know how lucky you are that you're not here, because if you were, I'd brain you with a turkey leg."

"Well," Martha remarked to the empty room, watching Emily stomp away, "I suppose there's all sorts of progress."

All three leaves had been added to the already massive dining room table, and two smaller tables had been set up in the entryway between the dining and living rooms. Silver platters and dishes piled with food lined two buffet tables, and everyone filled their plates, then found their assigned seats, saving Inez and the other kitchen helpers a lot of bother.

Emily sat with Joe, Jr. and Teddy and Max, as well

as Amber and Tripp, who had taken pity on her, so that Amber made sure to put their place cards alongside her sister.

"Max is Emily's date," Teddy said with a giggle, his hair still damp from the shower he and all the other "boys" had been forced to take before they could come to dinner. "Joe told me so."

"I'm not old enough to have a date," Max said with a seriousness that belied his years. "But if you'd help cut my meat, Aunt Emily, I'll play Nintendo with you after dessert."

Emily smiled at the boy, tousled his hair. "And *that's* a date, Max," she said. "Can it be one of those car racing games? I'm pretty good at those."

"Think you can beat me, do you?" Max sat back, crossed his arms over his small chest, sighed. "Women," he said, comically sighing and rolling his eyes.

Everyone at the table burst into laughter, the precocious Max having struck again, and Emily actually found the appetite she'd thought she'd lost the past two days.

She was just raising a forkful of stuffing to her mouth when Inez came into the dining room to say that there was a guest come to the back door.

"The kitchen door? Why not the front door?" Joe asked, half rising from his seat at the head of the table. "Who is it, Inez? Did he give you his name?"

"He says he came to the back door, hoping to be able to speak to you or Mrs. Colton. And he says his name is Atkins. Josh Atkins."

Emily's fork dropped onto her plate with a *clank*, then bounced onto the floor.

"Emily?" Amber asked, touching her sister's arm. "Honey, are you all right? You're white as a sheet."

"I'm fine, Amber," Emily heard herself say, knowing how strange her voice sounded to her own ears. "Excuse me. I—I want to get something out of my room."

"Emily, sit," Joe said, already heading for the kitchen. In moments he was back, Josh with him, dressed in stovepipe style jeans, a soft blue-and-green striped shirt, his tan suede coat unbuttoned, his black Stetson curled in his hands.

"Everybody, this is Josh Atkins," Joe said as he took up his place once more, standing behind his chair. "Josh, this is almost everybody. But we can do the introductions later, I think. I'm pretty sure the one you're looking for is over there, at the kiddie table."

"Yes, sir, thank you, sir," Josh said, and headed down the length of the table, straight at Emily, who kept her back turned even as she heard his boots on the parquet floor, his spurs jingling with each step he took. "Emily?"

She picked up her napkin, dabbed at the corners of her mouth, wishing her hands weren't shaking so badly. "Josh," she said, not turning around, not looking at him.

"Could we be more...private?" he asked, the intimate tone of his voice curling her toes inside her shoes.

"Why?" she asked, sitting tight, hanging on to her

anger. How dare he just show up, as if he had nothing better to do, so he might as well come by, see if there was any extra turkey.

"Emily..." Josh repeated, this time a warning tone invading his voice. She felt her chair being pulled out, and resisted the juvenile impulse to grab hold of the edge of the table.

She felt stupid, sitting there, her chair pulled away from the table, Joe, Jr. and Teddy and Max looking at her, eyes wide, then looking up at Josh. "Wow, cool," Max, a resident of Washington, D.C., said at last. "A real cowboy."

"Come on, Emily," Josh said, leaning down to whisper in her ear. "We need to talk."

No, they didn't. Because maybe he'd say he'd come back just to say goodbye. It was one thing, one awful thing, that he'd left. But what if he'd only come back to tell her he'd thought it all over, and he'd been right, there was no future for them. As long as he was gone, she could believe he might come back and tell her he loved her. But now he was here, and she was frightened, so very frightened.

And angry.

"Took your sweet time getting here, didn't you?" she heard herself ask him. "San Antonio was six days ago."

"You've been keeping tabs on me? How about that. Why, Emily? Tell me why. Oh, for crying out— Come here," Josh said, jamming his Stetson down hard on his head. Then he bent down, scooping Emily up and over his shoulder and headed back toward the door to the kitchen.

"Sit down, Rand, Drake," Meredith said, waving a hand toward her sons, who had risen from their chairs, ready to defend their sister. "River, you and Tripp and the rest of you, too. Can't you see everything's just fine?"

"Just fine?" Rand asked, subsiding into his chair. "You couldn't have proved that by me," he said as Josh stopped at the head of the table, looked down at Meredith. Emily squirmed against him, but she wasn't saying anything.

"Ma'am," Josh said, tipping his Stetson at Meredith.

"Maybe you'll be back in time for dessert," Meredith said, smiling up at him.

"Yes, ma'am, and thank you. I hope you'll excuse us now, ma'am, Senator?"

"You're going to tell her how it's going to be, aren't you, son?" Joe asked, smiling. "Good."

"Dad!" Emily exclaimed, lifting her head as Josh pushed open the swinging door, headed out through the kitchen. "How can you say such a thing? Josh, put me down! Put me down this instant. Josh, do you hear me, I said—"

The slamming of the kitchen door effectively cut off anything else Emily might have said, and moments later Inez pushed open the swinging door, poked her head into the dining room once more. "He took her outside and put her in his truck, and she didn't try to get out again. They're driving away now.''

''Thank you, Inez,'' Joe said, his wife's hand slipping into his, closing tight. ''Now how about some champagne? I think we've got some celebrating to do.''

Sixteen

It was quiet inside the cab of the truck as Josh steered it through the gates of the Hacienda de Alegria, onto the open road.

He looked over at Emily, secure inside her seat belt. ''Aren't you going to ask me where we're going?''

Emily sat, facing front, arms crossed over her chest. ''I can't. I'm not talking to you.''

''Oh, well, in that case—''

She cut him off. ''How could you *do* that to me? Come waltzing into the house—on Thanksgiving, no less, and right in the middle of dinner—and then just pick me up and carry me out of there?''

''Funny, I thought you weren't talking to me,'' Josh remarked, turning into the drive leading to Sophie and River's ranch house.

"I lied, so sue me, why don't you," Emily grumbled, then peered through the windshield. "This is Sophie's house. What are we doing at Sophie's house?"

Josh pulled the truck to a stop, cut the ignition. "We're borrowing it, with her permission, I might add. The cave was too far away."

"Borrow…? We're *borrowing* it?" Emily shook her head, trying to clear it. "And Sophie gave you permission? Oh, I don't believe it! Wait, yes I do. And she never said anything to me. She never said a single word!"

"Unlike her sister, who says she isn't going to say a single word, then starts talking a blue streak. Now, are you coming along willingly, Emily," he asked, holding up a ring of keys, "or am I going to have to carry you again?"

"River didn't know," Emily said, pretty much talking to herself as she climbed out of the cab, stepped onto the wide front porch of the house. "He was one of them standing up, ready to come to my rescue while Dad was throwing me to the wolves. Wolf," she corrected, glaring at Josh's back as he bent to insert the key in the front door.

Josh pushed open the door, reached inside against the wall to flip on the lights. "River didn't know, if River is Sophie's husband, which I'm assuming he is. Nobody knew. Nobody except Sophie, that is."

"How?" Emily asked, rubbing her arms against the chill as the warmth of the house reminded her she'd been dragged outside without her coat. "How did Sophie get in on this?"

"I met with her yesterday," Josh admitted, trying to stop looking at Emily, knowing he must look as if he wanted to eat her up, right now, before he had a chance to tell her, to explain. "I, well, I was here, and trying to figure out how to approach you. You're right, you know, there are one whole hell of a lot of Coltons, and most of them seem to be on the ranch right now."

"Yes, and you made one really *swell* first impression on all of them a few minutes ago," Emily said, sniffing. "I wouldn't be surprised if Max asks to take you home with him so he can drag you to school for show and tell."

Emily was pacing, striding back and forth across the large carpet, clenching and unclenching her hands.

Josh thought she looked magnificent.

"Are you going to let me tell you what you say you want to know, or not?" he asked after a few moments, and Emily stopped, glared at him, then finally subsided onto the couch. "Ah, that's better. I think."

"Tell me about Sophie," Emily said, looking at him, yet not quite looking at him, as if she didn't want to see too much of him if he might go away again. As if he'd ever go away again.

"I was parked at the side of the road, outside the gates, trying to figure out how I was going to be able to get you alone, talk to you, and Sophie drove up, parked behind me. I forgot that my license plate says RODEO RDR," he explained. "Anyway, your sister saw the license and figured out the rest."

"That sounds like Sophie," Emily said, nervously

pleating the folds of her soft navy wool skirt. "Go on."

Josh looked at the chairs, the couch, and then perched himself on the edge of the coffee table, close in front of Emily. "I told her my problem, she said surprise attacks always work best, and we came up with a plan. The Byde-A-Wee Motel just wouldn't cut it, you know, and I needed to be able to take you someplace private. Sophie did say that she hoped I'd talk fast and that you'd listen, wouldn't throw anything, because she really likes her knickknacks, or whatever it is she called them. Now, are we going to go around and around about this, or can I tell you I'm an idiot? A big, stupid, hardheaded idiot."

Emily turned her head, so that he could only see her in profile. "Emily?"

"You're not an idiot," she said, so softly he had to lean forward to hear her. "Toby did love me, and that can't be changed. Toby's dead, and that can't be changed, either."

"True," Josh said, nodding his head. "All true. And for a while, Emily, that's all I could see. But I see more than that now."

She turned back to face him. "What do you mean? What's changed?"

"Nothing," Josh said, a slight, sad smile on his face.

"Oh," Emily said, trying to rise, but Josh's hands shot out, pushing her back down onto the couch.

"Emily, Toby is gone. I love him, will always love him, but he's gone. We can't change that, and we can't live the rest of our lives denying what's between us. That's no way at all to remember the best brother a man ever had, the best friend you ever had. Toby wouldn't want me to mourn him forever, and he didn't save you so that you could spend the rest of your life alone. That we met, that we...loved, is a good thing, a very good thing. I think Toby would be happy for both of us."

"Are—" Emily stopped, sighed. "Are you sure?"

"Am I sure I love you?" Josh asked, reaching for her, pulling her into his arms. "Sweetheart, I've never been so sure of anything in my life. What worries me is if you'll want anything to do with a soon-to-be-retired rodeo rider who wants nothing more than to marry you, settle down and raise a bunch of kids."

Emily's shoulders, which she had been holding stiff, relaxed, her entire expression relaxed, and tears flooded her eyes. "Martha was right," she said, the unfamiliar name making him frown slightly. "She said I could survive without you, that I could come to terms with everything that's happened, and heal myself. And I've done it. I could go on without you."

Josh shook his head. "I don't understand."

Emily's smile deepened, broadened. "Oh, that's all right, darling. You don't have to understand. You just need to know that, even though I *could* go on without you, I don't want to. I love you, Josh. I've loved you forever."

"How has she been?" Meredith asked the doctor as they stood outside the lounge area where the patients/inmates met with visitors.

The doctor shrugged. "I think we've hit on a good

combination of drugs, Mrs. Colton, but your sister can be very inventive in finding ways of not taking them. Still, she's been on her best behavior since your phone call yesterday, telling us about Dr. Hanford here."

Jewel Mayfair Baylor Hanford stepped forward a pace and smiled at the doctor. "It was good of you to arrange this meeting so quickly, Doctor," she said. "I know I should have waited, but after so many years, all I could think to do was find the fastest way here from Ohio."

Meredith squeezed Jewel's hand. The two had met at the ranch, Joe having sent his private plane for her niece only two days after Austin had been satisfied Jewel was definitely Patsy's daughter. Jewel had left her husband and two young children behind in Medford, and planned to fly home again that same evening.

She looked so much like her mother, and like Meredith. There had been no need for DNA tests, and there certainly had been no more questions once Jewel and Meredith had come face-to-face. This was her niece, her sister's daughter. Dr. Jewel Hanford, child psychologist.

"And you're all right with this?" the doctor asked Jewel. "I must say that I was heartened to hear of your background in psychology. It should make things easier all around, although I'm sure nothing about these next few minutes is going to be particularly easy."

"Which is why I'd like to get them over with as soon as possible," Jewel said, and Meredith smiled at the hint of velvet steel in her niece's voice. Patsy may have made a terrible mess of her own life, but Jewel was not Patsy. She was strong, yet loving. Highly intelligent and ready to accept whatever she found once that last door between herself and her biological mother was finally opened.

"Yes, yes of course," the doctor stammered, and inserted a key into the lock, then stood back, allowing Meredith to enter the lounge ahead of him.

"Patsy?" Meredith began, looking at her sister, who was standing at the barred window, her back to the room. She'd lost more weight, and the drab blue wraparound dress hung on her thin shoulders. "Patsy, Jewel's here with me."

"Saw her," Patsy bit out, still with her back turned. "Saw the two of you, down there, when you got out of the car. Now get her the hell out of here."

Meredith looked to Jewel in confusion, hurting for the rejected child.

"It's all right, Mrs. Colton," Jewel assured her. "Maybe if you just give us a few minutes alone? Doctor? Is that all right with you?"

The doctor looked at her, then finally nodded his head. "We'll be right outside, and there's a glass in the window, so we can observe."

"Thank you, Doctor," Jewel said, then smiled reassuringly at her aunt.

Meredith and the doctor retreated to the other side of the door, both of them watching through the wired glass as Jewel stood where she was and Patsy remained, back still turned, at the window.

"What's going on?" Meredith asked. "I don't understand, Doctor. All these years, all Patsy has wanted was to find her daughter.''

''Yes, and now the fantasy has become reality, and she's too ashamed to face that daughter. I said the new combination of antipsychotic drugs seemed to be working. Unfortunately, they're working well enough for your sister to have enough of a grasp on reality to know that her daughter may just reject her now, and with good reason.''

''Oh, poor Patsy,'' Meredith said, blinking back tears. ''And I thought we'd done a good thing.''

Meredith watched as Jewel slowly took one step forward, then another. Jewel was talking, although Meredith couldn't make out the words, but just the low, reassuring tone of her voice.

Jewel advanced until she was standing directly behind Patsy, and Meredith could see the bone-white of her sister's knuckles as they held on to the bars at the window.

And then, slowly, Patsy turned around. The look on her face made Meredith gasp, for never had she seen such love in her sister's eyes, such hope.

Patsy reached out, laid her palm against Jewel's face, and Jewel lifted her hand, pressed it on top of her mother's. The pair stood there, just that way, for long moments, before Jewel put her arms around her mother and held her close.

Meredith searched in her purse for a handkerchief, then turned away, to give her sister some privacy. ''What now, Doctor? What now?''

''I don't know, Mrs. Colton. I'd like to say that Miss Portman will recover, but I think we both know that's impossible. Drugs or not, she's slowly slipping away from us, into a world that shields her from reality and all she's done. The impersonation, the murders, everything. She'll never leave here, Mrs. Colton, and in time, she'll be content to stay, and forget the rest of the world even exists. I'm sorry, but you should know that. Dr. Hanford should know that.''

Meredith looked through the glass, to see Patsy and Jewel sitting side-by-side, Jewel showing Patsy the same family photographs she'd shown her earlier in the day, showing Patsy her grandchildren. Meredith felt her heart break and swell at the same time, her happiness tinged with sadness, yet hope conquering all.

''I think she knows, Doctor. But for now she's found her biological mother and two half brothers. She's found them, and an entire family who will love her and welcome her and her family into our lives. And, strange as it may sound when I say it, with Jewel in our lives now, I've sort of gotten my sister back, haven't I? So you see, there's a happy ending here, of sorts. Isn't there, Doctor?''

''Oh, I just love this dress, Emily,'' Sophie said, holding the flowing skirt of her deep burgundy bridesmaid's dress and twirling about in a circle. ''I'm so glad if you were only going to have one attendant that you picked me.''

''And you're just lucky I've forgiven you for not telling me Josh was here for a full day and night before he came to see me,'' Emily told her, not for the first time. ''Here, help me with this necklace, please. Aunt Sybil says I have to wear it, but I can't manage the clasp. I'm *so* nervous."

"With Aunt Sybil in the house, who isn't?" Sophie joked. "Mom is sure she'll set fire to the place with one of her cigarettes. Hold still," she went on as Emily bent her knees so that Sophie could drape the antique pearls around her neck. "There, that does it, and not a moment too soon, because here comes Dad to walk you down the aisle."

Joe Colton had knocked on the open door to Emily's room, stepping inside with all the ease of a man going to face a firing squad. "You're all decent in here, I hope?" he asked, nervously averting his eyes. Meredith had sent him in here, and he wasn't sure he was up to it, up to seeing Emily in her wedding gown.

"Oh, would you look at him, Emily? Dad, you're blushing. Here, look at Emily."

Joe sighed, then turned his head and looked at his daughter. He saw the little girl who had held his hand, crawled into his lap, said his whiskers "tick-licked" her when she kissed him good night. "You're beautiful, Emily," he said, his voice catching in his throat, his face just as red as Meredith had predicted it would be above the tight collar of his tuxedo shirt. "And everybody's waiting, so let's get on with this, okay?"

Sophie whispered in Emily's ear, "Our dad, one big soft, squishy marshmallow. Come on, Emily, Josh is waiting, and I don't think he's a patient man."

Emily saw her not very patient man as she walked into the living room of the Hacienda de Alegria on her father's arm. He stood with the minister, just in front of the huge fireplace, wearing a tuxedo he'd just bought and new snakeskin cowboy boots that had come courtesy of the boot company whose products he endorsed. He looked tall, and handsome, and scared out of his mind.

Emily smiled at him, and he looked at her, blinked, took one involuntary step forward before waiting for the small procession to make its way past the rented chairs, then held out his hand to her.

Joe took Emily's hand and placed it in Josh's as the minister asked, "Who gives this woman's hand in marriage?" He answered, "Her mother and I," before joining Meredith in the first row of chairs.

"You're the most beautiful woman in the world," Josh whispered as he and Emily turned toward the minister. "And I'm the world's luckiest man."

Emily and Josh planned to fly to New Mexico in the morning, rejoining the rodeo tour as Josh made his farewell appearances, which would last for the next few months. They could have waited until the spring to marry, but the idea of being separated again, even for a moment, weighed heavy in their decision.

Emily stood to one side of the small, cleared spot that served as a dance floor, and watched as Josh danced to piped-in music with a clearly infatuated Tatania, knowing it would soon be time for them to leave, as they had booked the bridal suite at a hotel close to the airport.

"Tatania's having a good time," Martha said, her face glowing with motherly pride. "I think she's danced with every man here, the little minx."

"How is she feeling?" Emily asked, moving her

weight from one foot to the other, as her new white satin high heels were beginning to pinch. All she wanted now was to get out of this gown and into comfortable clothes, all with the hope that Josh would soon get her out of them again.

"Better," Martha answered, looking at her daughter. "But I'm so glad that Blake agreed that I could bring her home with me, to our new home. There are so many children down with that flu at Hopechest. I'm glad she isn't around all those germs."

"Yes, Rebecca says they've got their hands full right now. The flu, you say? So that's what it is?"

"So far, that's what it is," Martha told her, sighing. "Even though she's getting rest and lots of chicken soup, don't you think it strange that Tatania got so much better once she was away from Hopechest? Oh, never mind. Blake's on it. We'll have an answer soon."

"I'm sure you will," Emily said, kissing Martha's cheek. "Have I told you lately how grateful I am that you were here for me, to listen to me, to be my friend?"

"That's a two-way street, Emily. The Coltons have changed my life, and I'm eternally grateful."

"Mom and Dad. They did it all. Aren't they wonderful? What time is it, Martha?"

"Are you thinking the same thing I am?" Martha asked, coming to stand beside Emily. "Dinner's over, the cake's been cut, you've tossed your bouquet, which Tatania caught, and Josh threw the garter, which Max caught, then promptly stuck on his head. I'd say it's time, wouldn't you?"

"Yes, Martha, I would," Emily agreed, looking toward the dance floor, where her mother and father swayed together, Meredith's head on Joe's shoulder. "I'll alert the minister."

"And I'll go find Inez, who's probably loading another tray of goodies for everyone. After all, she's the one who first gave me the idea."

A few minutes later, Rand crossed to the fireplace and signaled that River turn off the stereo system, then clapped his hands to gain everyone's attention.

"Ladies and gentlemen," he said, smiling at the small company of friends and family, "we've had a lovely wedding, and the family thanks you all for coming. We've welcomed a new member to our family today and heard him and Emily exchange the vows that will sustain them through the years, the good times and bad, the happy times and the sad. Vows," he continued as his wife, Lucy, joined him in front of the fireplace, a bouquet of tiny pink rosebuds in her hands, "spoken from the heart. We say them when we marry, we live them as we grow together, move together through those years."

"Oh, my, he's very good," Martha whispered in Emily's ear as Josh came to join them. "I just know I'm going to cry."

"Mom? Dad?" Rand went on, motioning for her parents to come forward, join him. "We weren't there when you said those vows to each other, but we've seen how well you've lived them. We'd all be proud, and grateful, if you'd renew those vows now, in front of your children and your grandchildren, who weren't around the first time."

"Oh, Rand, no," Meredith said, burying her head against Joe's shoulder as Lucy handed her the bouquet.

"Mom, I'm the oldest," Rand reminded her jokingly. "The way I've heard the joke, that means I'll choose your nursing home. So maybe you'd better keep me happy."

"Joe?" Meredith asked, looking up at her husband as the minister, still nibbling on a bit of Inez's cake, made his way to the fireplace. "Should we?"

"If you'll have me, Meredith," Joe told her, raising both her hands to his lips, kissing them. "But if you want me down on my knees, to propose again, just remember I may not be able to get up again."

And so, with laughter, and also with tears, the Colton family gathered around the fireplace, gathered around the two people whose dreams, whose vision, had built the Hacienda de Alegria, the House of Joy, and filled it with children of their bodies, children of their hearts.

"I, Joseph Colton, take thee, Meredith Portman..."

"I, Meredith Portman, take thee, Joseph Colton..."

"For better, for worse, in good times and in bad."

"...for richer, for poorer, in sickness and in health."

"...to love, and to cherish, for all the days of our lives..."

* * * * *

Don't miss the next story
from Silhouette's

LONE STAR COUNTRY CLUB:
STROKE OF FORTUNE

by Christine Rimmer
Available June 2002
Turn the page for an excerpt
from this exciting romance...!

Chapter One

The two golf carts reached the ninth tee at a little after eight that Sunday morning in late May. Tyler Murdoch and Spence Harrison rode in the first cart. Flynt Carson and Dr. Michael O'Day, the blind fourth they'd picked up at the clubhouse when Luke Callaghan didn't show, took up the rear.

It was one of those rare perfect mornings, the temperature in the seventies, the sky a big blue bowl, a wispy cloud or two drifting around up there. Somewhere in the trees overhead, a couple of doves cooed at each other.

When the men emerged from under the cover of the oaks, the fairway, still glistening a little from its early-morning watering, was so richly green it hardly seemed real. A deep, true green, Flynt Carson thought. Like Josie's eyes...

Flynt swore under his breath. He'd been vowing for nearly a year that he'd stop thinking about her. Still, her name always found some way to come creeping into his mind.

"What did you say?" Michael O'Day pulled their cart to a stop on the trail right behind spence and Tyler. "I think I caught the meaning, but I missed the exact words." He slanted Flynt a knowing grin.

Flynt ordered his mind to get back where it belonged—on his game. "Just shaking my head over that last hole. If I'd come out of the sand a little better, I could have parred it. No doubt about it, my sand wedge needs work."

Michael chuckled. "Hey, at least you—"

And right then Flynt heard the kind of sound a man *shouldn't* hear on the golf course. He put up a hand, though Michael had already fallen silent.

The two in the front cart must have heard it, too. They were turning to look for the source as it came again: a fussy little cry.

"Over there," Spence said. He pointed toward the thick hedge that partially masked a groundskeeper's shed about thirty yards from them.

A frown etched a crease between Michael's black eyebrows. "Sounds like a—"

Spence was already out of the lead cart. "Damn it, I don't believe it."

Neither did Flynt. He blinked. And he looked again.

But it was still there: a baby carrier, the kind that doubles as a car seat, tucked in close to the hedge. And in the car seat—wrapped in a fluffy pink blanket, waving tiny fists and starting to wail—was a baby.

A baby. A baby *alone.* On the ninth tee of the Lone Star Country Club's Ben Hogan-designed golf course.

"What the hell kind of idiot would leave a baby on the golf course?" Tyler Murdoch asked the question of no one in particular. He took off after Spence. Flynt and Michael fell in right behind.

Midway between the carts and the squalling infant, all four men slowed. The baby cried louder and those tiny fists flailed.

The men—Texans all, tall, narrow-hipped, broad-shouldered and proud—stopped dead, two in front, two right behind, about fifteen feet from the yowling child. Three of those men had served in the Gulf War together. Each of those three had earned the Silver Star for gallantry in action. The fourth, Michael O'Day, was perhaps the finest cardiac surgeon in the Lone Star State. He spent his working life fighting to save lives in the operating room—and most of the time, he won. Flynt's own father, Ford Carson, was a living testament to the skill and steely nerves of Dr. O'Day.

Not a coward in the bunch.

But that howling baby stopped them cold. To the world they might be heroes, but they were also single men. And childless. Not a one knew what the hell to do with a crying infant.

Another several edgy seconds passed, with the poor kid getting more worked up, those little arms pumping wildly, the fat little face crumpled in misery, getting very red.

Then Tyler said, "Spence." He gestured with a tight nod to the left. "I'll go right. We'll circle the shed and rendezvous around the back. Then we'll check out the interior."

"Gotcha." The two started off, Tyler pausing after a few steps to advise over his shoulder, "Better see to that kid."

Flynt resisted the urge to argue, *No way.* You *deal with the baby.* We'll *reconnoiter the shed.* But he'd missed his chance and he knew it. He and Michael were stuck with the kid.

Michael looked grim. Flynt was certain his own expression mirrored the doctor's. But what damn choice did they have? Someone had to take care of the baby.

"Let's do it," he said bleakly, already on his way again toward the car seat and its unhappy occupant.

As his shadow fell across the child, the wailing stopped. The silence, to Flynt, seemed huge. And wonderful, after all that screaming.

The baby blinked up at him. A girl, Flynt guessed—the blanket, after all, *was* pink. Her bright blue eyes seemed to be seeking, straining to see him looming above her. And then she gave up. She shut those eyes and opened that tiny mouth and let out another long, angry wail.